Long Before the Next War

Long Before the Next War

Tony Anthony

Cedar Crest Books

Cedar Crest Books
Natick, MA USA
www.cedarcrestbooks.com

Long Before the Next War
by Tony Anthony

Cover Design: Iguana
Book Design: Laura A. Nagel

First Printing – September 2016

ISBN: 978-0-910291-15-6

To Walter Jackson

Zabriski folds the Hulk
Unfolds Spider Man.

His eyes are red
And shining mirrors like
The gleaming side of the Chevrolet
In the snapshot
He carries.

The Chevy sits
Its left side to you
Beside the house in Maine.

Gablinger is behind the wheel
Resting a can of Bud
On the dash.

His younger brother
Snapped the shot
With the Instamatic
His father gave him
To take to Vietnam.

—Two days ago
Gablinger snapped a shot
Of a gook he shot
On automatic.

The back is off the Instamatic.
The film is wet
Probably ruining the shot of the gook.

—We fold the camera parts
With the wet film
Inside Gablinger's poncho.

Macaroni and cheese
Dark sky with supper.

Under the leaves I am stupid and stupefied. Forgetful almost to the point of insanity. Most of the promises we believed we were here for—I have lost now.

> Part of the ridiculous sky—
> Part of the malevolent sky—
> Part of the violent sky.

Something's wrong. The sky is too beautiful above this hellhole. But we are stuck to the ground. Something is happening but we're too low in the ranks to know. Small things scare us at our level. We live by rumor and the littlest, most innocent scraps from the majors and colonels....
We live with the shit scared out of us.
Is it needed for us to be subjected to
such treatment?
I see my feet for the first time in
three weeks.
There is black fungus between my toes.
Is there somebody I should ask?
What good would it do?
My feet'll fall off—but me, I'll live.

Dark my dreams, white the light I choose to write in. Dark my thoughts, attacking fearsome figures, berserk like a runaway trumpet, which I can't stop playing. I am the quiet portrait of a purely singular figure: my face, my set of arms and legs, static energy.

Family portrait: my uncle's farm, with him, my mother, me, my aunt, my sister, my father, standing all in a row.

Who was it took the picture? I wonder. I've got shades on—and a beret. My father is holding a camera in his hand. My sister looks pregnant. Everybody is smiling. Even me.

I roll up my pant leg. One leech sucking blood. I watch him, then lie back to sleep. Too tired to make a bed. Too tired for anything but a dream:

A very sexy, long-legged school teacher stands in the center of a classroom, holding a piece of chalk in her hand. She has short-shorts on. Tall black boots. Stiletto heels. Sex magazine style. But no face. No face. "I shall not hit Johnny," is written in rows all up and down the blackboard. A picture of George Washington is on the wall. An American flag, too. The teacher lies down on the floor. I make love to her. She still has no face.

Two incoming sniper rounds. I crouch sideways, not sitting up, pulling on my boots. I take my weapon off safe. I lie still. No more fire. Harassment. Nobody hit. Go to sleep.

We are still alive.

I swear to myself I am going to live.

I swear I am going to die.

Can't make up my mind.

I have no mind.

**Full moon tonight
Charlie won't fight.**

A picture's in my pocket. A blonde girl, beautiful, with thin arms sits on a light brown horse. She has wide eyes and high cheekbones. She has a red scarf wrapped about her. Around her head, she wears a bandana. She is smiling and I guess I'm in love. But I can't see her picture because I can't light a light. I picture her in my mind but it's not the same.

I'll wait until morning and maybe have a dream.
What is that name I thought up for her?
I can't remember now.
Will I ever get to meet her?
It's just a picture from a magazine.
I wonder about seeing her in a bright bikini with
a weapon in her hand.

No thought or realization of the future—
I shall return as ten thousand dogs.

It must be the ascetic life that postulates and makes possible the true happiness, the true good. Goddamnit, I can see that. Hell, why don't I go and buy a robe of saffron silk?

To study and fulfill the mountains and trees and the mountain's breeze, I must rid the ego of sisters and brothers and mothers and fathers and I can feel it happening. With no publicity, with only smirks at other bearded idiots with no hair, with only the Tonight Show's furtive glances at audience women. All these things cannot live in peace together. If I could forget my pairs of shoes and cars and watches and all the symbols that I cling to—then freedom would be so easy.

I must forget love. Forget all these incredible objects to which I've whispered reverently the words, "I love you." I have to dump you—rid myself of you, Marianne, Wonder Girl, bulbous watermelons floating under college t-shirts. My first feel. The way you grabbed my wrists and pulled my sweaty cold palms up under your shirt. The way I climbed you in the front seat and then in a frenzy dragged you across the beach and dove on you like someone diving into a fresh morning sea.

I must find the way to forget you...all.

In war, motion is meaningless.
Picture in my wallet: A Dutch craftsman sits
on a solitary chair carving wooden shoes.

PFC Spellbinder with his poor fucking name—he stares with ball bearing eyes at our tactical map. What the hell is he trying to figure out? Poor fucker. Poor fucker. We are not going to help him because he's got to learn, and if he doesn't ALL of our shit is going to be out. He must know we can't help him. Who the hell can we help here? Who? Not anybody, not me, not a word of advice for home. I never write letters. A letter is an endless supply of the same words, reused.

I can't help any fucking body so I'm writing
no more letters.

No talk today. No talk.

A.M. resupply chopper-popper brings us last night's supper for breakfast. Got a letter from some aunt who I don't even know. Only a picture she's cut out of some paper. Caption: "Sooooo Good. A young Vietnamese girl is watched by a smiling friend as she takes a puff of a cigarette. The girls are visiting Marble Mountain shrine in Danang. In South Vietnam it is not unusual for children to smoke."

My aunt's caption: "Hi Warren. So you see we get the news here, too. She is a cutie."

Maybe I'll die today.
Good chance of it.

Picture of Leigh Taylor-Young with flowers in her hair in a sexy hippie-chick, see-through shirt. Somebody give me strength to not give up today. I draw a heart in ballpoint pen on her shoulder. But it comes out more like an apple. My hand is not too steady anymore.

Rotten meat for breakfast.

I wonder what kind of animal they killed to get it. A rat, I guess. I spit it out. Breakfast for a thousand ants. Everybody gives me their coffee rations. I'm the company coffee freak. That's my breakfast and lunch for today. Plus, one thousand cigarettes, which I collect instead of stamps. Fucking Army knows how to treat a guy right.

Maybe I'll try laughing in my sleep.
I could get a job as Jonathan Winters when I
get out.
I forgot. I'm going to die today…

Pretty Buddha Mountain. Has got a top as flat as a table. Well, time to get to work. No time to think about a mountain. I guess we got to blow its shit away. Good day.

The mountain (instructions):

We're gonna blow its shit away.

We're gonna blow its shit away.

(kids are jumping rope back in elementary
school, singing my song for me)

Nothing is better about me for being here and coming in contact with different tortures and different deaths. Dying here is no nobler than dying in New York City. Life is more disastrous in war but death is just the same.

I ask you for the connections of your life, you upon the horse, you whose neck contains so much hurt, you whose body has been mistreated, you who have been the quietest girl at the dance at Sarah Lawrence, you who rode back with me from Millbrook. You who I imagined would have put a hand upon my neck to soothe me when I suffered to come to this place. You who I know as no one. You who I can touch only in imagination. You who I love. You who I am at war for—you for whom I am not the hero ever expected. Understand. Understand, Goddamn you and the shapes you have taken—the skinny fucking princess from Boston, the aged beauty from Coconut Grove, the perfection of Priscilla, the suffering you do as Jane—the way you come to me in music, the way you ask me to fight for you, the way you hide in all of your environs (the secrets to yourself), the changes of shape, the sexes you turn into, the smiles you forget, the way you hide your face in shadow, a thought I have placed for you on the cold ledge of living in time—

The most embarrassing moment of life is saved for asking you this and you know it, have known it before I've begun. You have thrown me the world in place of yourself and the hate I might work up is making you happier. It becomes you beautifully, doesn't it? You in New Canaan, you on the ride back from Bedford, you in Vermont, skiing, you in the islands, you in all the places I've yet to see you. I'll travel to see your games in as many forms as I can—only to, in the end, in the ways I can, perform for you.

You want me to give up and do funny things in place of trying to get at you...I feel that sometimes I come close enough to scare you—yes, I can see the letters that make up the words that make you afraid. Just as touches to your virginal heart make your bronze vagina start to crack.

("When the Moon Comes Over the
Mountain," sing the jump-rope girls)
The cold leech dies full of blood.
Where do I go from here?

The place feels comfortable—
Not good—not good...

Fear and worry. Worry and fear. Two things
nobody should have. Not a grunt going out
on patrol.
It just is what it is.
No control.
Not fate.
It will be what it will be.
(the little girls in kindergarten sing this song)

Out on this peninsula called Batangan. Sounds like a
place where a battle could take place—a firefight.

I walk with my head down, my eyes facing the ground.
Every little leaf poses a threat. All the fear instilled in us in
training.

"Step on an innocent leaf and the wrong one
will blow you up, troop!"
(I can hear the drill sergeant's voice)
"A candy wrapper. A piece of string." God
knows, you don't touch a piece of string!

But all I'm seeing is this sandy trail with pine needles
too thin to be hiding anything. We're humping through a
pine forest. With trees that are small and spaced far apart.
Nothing can hide behind them—not even a skinny gook!

Reminds me of the forests in South Carolina where we
trained, where we knew if a Vietnamese popped out and
attacked us it was gonna be a member of the training cadre
and he was gonna be firing blanks—not real bullets.

Pssst. A bullet passes by. Was that a bullet? A live round?
I look around and everyone in front of me is on the ground.

I hear, "Get down!" And they're yelling at me.

Are we in a war? A battle? A firefight?

I get the fuck down.

We wait and wait. A few more bullets pass by. Nothing serious. No serious injuries. No serious death. Then we're back on our feet, humping once again for another hour and the sandy soil of Batangan feels like summers on the beach in Long Island when I was a little kid. A very safe place.

Where nobody was ever gonna shoot at me.

And we—my sister and I—would play in the sand by the water chasing fiddler crabs. "See them run!" (the children squeal) "See them run!"

We stop before we get to the ville. I've seen it on the map—the squad leader showed it to us—all colored in pink. All commies. All Viet Cong. All bad guys. We have permission to shoot. Permission to kill.

We're lined up behind a rice paddy dike, facing a cluster of grass-roofed huts (just like in the pictures) (just like the fake Vietnamese villages at Fort Jackson).

Holy shit—and here they are! Three tiny little Vietnamese guys about 50 yards away, dressed in black pajamas with straw, conical hats.

HOLY FUCK!

I PULL THE TRIGGER! I hear a pop.

It's my M16. I'm not the only one firing. I hear everyone else join in. The three figures run. They're running from right to left. "Lead in front of the first one," the drill sergeant told us back in South Carolina. PULL THE TRIGGER AGAIN. HOLY FUCK! I see him go down. He looks like he tripped or bent down to pick up something. Only he never gets back up.

BLAM BLAM. THANK YOU MA'AM. The other two

run off to our left—like they're trying to get off the Tee Vee screen. Shoot again. Some other guys this time. Not me. I'm done. I've done what I've done.

We get word (that's the way it's said when an order is passed down the line). The word is: "Advance. Move forward. Into the village."
HOLY SHIT! THIS IS TOO FUCKING REAL!
A young boy is on the ground. His hat fell off. It's nowhere to be found. His shirt is soaked in blood where the bullet went in through his chest and out through his arm.
(I will say that over and over in my head for
the next thousand years)
He's only about fourteen. Just a kid.
Just a boy.
The sergeant's on the radio. "Three enemy
KIA's," he says in a monotone voice.
"Outskirts of Son Tra."
(sounds like a novel somebody wrote)
Someone picks through the boy's clothing. Someone else pokes him with the muzzle of a gun. I guess to see if he's still alive. But the boy looks like a dead fish that flew up out of the water. Only he's not flopping around. Some of his blood is staining the pure white sand. Someone reaches in the pockets of the boy's pants and pulls out some coins. And smiles. "VC currency," he smiles again. So everything's all right. Because the boy had the right kind of money (or the wrong kind).

This is what the enemy looks like
Not some evil soldier with scars all over
his face
But a young boy with some coins in his pocket
Who happens to have lived in a village colored

18

pink on the map
Son Tra
Sounds like a song

I pull the trigger
To shoot my gun
(that feels like a toy)
A bullet flies out
It hits a little boy
I keep thinking that over and over....I know it's slow sui-
cide.
    (I hear the girls' chorus in elementary school
    singing my suicide song)

    Jaspon has a poncho.
    We spread it over the three of us.
    I feel the folly and me both, sharing my orange monk's
robes. It was known and done in such perfection when
chance, thinner than a hair, turned to say goodbye with the
supreme sadness of lost youth.
    Now I offer you...the colors of death.

**The girl with no voice—
She has no choice, she has no choice.**

The captain, the lieutenant, two guys from the platoon and me all pile into the captain's jeep and he drives us into Quang Ngai in search of some whores. He thinks he knows of this certain place and we others don't quite believe him—but it turns out he does. We go down an alleyway. I take my weapon off safe because it's a little too narrow and dark, and I've never been to a Vietnamese whorehouse before. I'm just hoping that it won't be as funky as the place in Columbia, South Carolina—the Princess Hotel where the whores were all older than somebody's mother, and were somebody's mothers or the wives of husbands that never returned from Nam and had to support the kids and got all fat and smelly and had to wear too much perfume to cover up the stink from their perspiration.

But the whores in Quang Ngai don't look like whores. They are nice young girls that happen to have no families, which is not uncommon in Vietnam. Mama San sits us down in old plastic American webbed beach chairs from some PX. And she offers us beers and Cokes for two dollars. The girls come in through a blanket that is hung in a doorway by safety pins.

I pick a young, very innocent-looking one. "She has no voice," Mama San smiles at me. I could say something cool like, "What does it matter for what we're gonna do?" but I don't and I'm glad I don't. I smile and say, "That's okay, I don't mind," as the girl named Vin (which I know is French for "wine") leads me off behind another blanket to where there is a damp old mattress lying on top of a military cot. I sit down and she pulls a bowl of soapy water (a bed pan, I guess) out from under the cot. She takes off her pajamas and squats down and makes a big deal out of dipping herself up and down in the soapy water and then shows me she's clean in the pussy.

When you're with someone with no voice, it's hard to say anything yourself, so I don't. She undoes my pants and makes me hard and just sits down on it and in two minutes it's over and I smile and she smiles.

We don't even kiss.

When I walk back out into the room with webbed chairs Mama San offers me another coke. This time I have a beer.

It isn't much fun at all.

**The chopper floor is cold
And I am getting old.**

It's 0630 hours and it's damp and foggy. The chopper is taking us to an LZ farther west. "Landing Zone Baldy" is its name.

First we fly high. About 3,000 feet. Then after a while we low-level. Just above the treetops. We do this because this is NVA Land and it's safer to fly low, so Charlie can't hear us coming.

My feet dangle from the edge of the chopper floor. I have this thought, that if I just slide myself out and land in a big, soft tree then I can go back to sleep.

The door gunner is already half-asleep. His head droops forward like it could fall off. Only his chin against his chest prevents it.

The chopper rises and lowers over trees of different heights like a ship riding waves on the sea.

We see bright green smoke up ahead, much brighter than the green of the trees. The chopper overflies the LZ. The gunner's eyes open. He watches the tree line intently. We were told this might be a hot LZ.

We draw no fire. The chopper doubles back, tilting way back on its tail. Then it settles down quickly to the ground blowing the green smoke away to all sides.

We jump down to relieve the men who are waiting.

Here goes nothing again, I think, when my feet hit Vietnam....

During his guard, Catchahorse wakes me up: "Listen, you've gotta hear this, man! You just won't believe it!" I follow him. We crawl to his position near a rock. He's very smart that way—finding a rock to hide behind.

"You have to be real, real quiet, then you can hear it," he

whispers in my ear. "It's Joan Baez."

Coming from the tree line, which is just a darker shade of black in the blackness in front of us, we hear a woman's voice on a cheap record player. It's *Where Have all the Flowers Gone* and it sounds faint and creepy drifting out of the dark.

Someone opens up with an M60 machine gun at the sound. Then another position shoots a few bursts with M16's.

Catchahorse and I just sit and listen. When the song ends, we hear the needle scratch across the record. Then it plays again. Every five minutes or so somebody gets pissed off and lets go a few bursts.

It takes more than an hour before the music stops.

A cry for help—
I need your picture, I need your picture, I need your picture.

Dark haired girl:

Where are you when my limbs are heavy, when my boots are weights?

I remember the whiteness of your thighs when you removed your stockings at the movies.

I remember the soft wetness when my finger moved inside you for the first time.

Do you remember me...still?

**All about
Motherfucking death.**

Division Command radios for our brigade chaplain to take a bird back to the rear today to the airbase at Chu Lai. A planeload of men just leaving for Stateside crashed on takeoff at the end of the runway. Everybody aboard was killed and there aren't enough chaplains in Chu Lai to perform all the necessary rites.

Later, when he's back, Chaplain tells me the plane never got off the ground—it just started spinning, then flipped over and crashed and burned. Everybody was pretty much turned to charcoal. Chaplain says they just lined up the dog tags on the runway and prayed for the men's souls.

This is a big deal to Chaplain. He's got a shit job. No more shit job than anyone else though.

On the side of a dirt hill on the outskirts of Quang Ngai, soldiers, of which I am one, guard Vietnamese men, women and children within concertina wire. Some of the Vietnamese men, women and children dig up a burial ground. The sound of women crying is constant. One woman holds her face in her hands. She squats and her toes curl over the edge of an open grave.

Two bearded men dig through the red earth. Suddenly one lifts a handful of white sand which means something: maybe they're close to the body. A murmur passes through the crowd gathered around the tiny rectangular hole. It is only four feet long and two or three feet deep when the old men clear the remaining red dirt. Soon the entire bottom of the grave is white. More children gather and every one of the faces stare expectantly at the sand. The craggy, work-worn hands of the two men finger gently through the grave bottom.

Two teenage girls intently weave a basket of reeds. As one finishes securing the last corner, the other spreads a lining of silk over the inside, folding it around the edges. The small pairs of hands have fashioned this coffin to fit the size of the grave.

The two men crowd into the rear of the small hole. The girls place the basket at the lip. The white sand is meticulously transferred onto the floor of the basket. In the hole, the outline of a tiny figure forms. The small bones are moved from the grave to the new coffin and soon a few elderly orange-clad Buddhists arrive to oversee the somber procession to the coffin's new place of rest. The women cry loudly now. The children continue to gaze in awe at the spectacle. Some, easily tired with so many adult tears, laugh and play.

The procession of the Buddhist priests weaves between the olive green forms of the soldiers guarding them with their rifles. Women gather around the new grave, weeping.

Page 42 in my Vietnamese Phrase Book:

Entering a Village

This village is surrounded.	Lang nay bi bao vay.
Bring me the village chief.	Dan xa truoung.
How many V.C. are there?	Co bao nhieu Viet Cong?
Where are the weapons hidden?	Nhung sung giau dau?
Where are the tunnels?	Nhung duong ham o dau?
Where are the booby traps?	Nhung ba no o dau?
Come outside.	Ta ngoai.
Enter first.	Vao truoc.
When was the attack?	Tan cong xay ra bao gio?
How many villagers were killed?	Bao nhieu ngudi lang bi chet?
How many V.C. were killed?	Bao nhieu Viet Cong bit chet?
Is this trail safe?	Duong mon nay co nguy hiem khong?

Toi muon ngu—I want to sleep, is my thought.

Hot, steaming leaves
John and Yoko, John and Yoko.

I see a spider six inches across and Rodriguez sees it too. The spider is above us on his web as big as a human house. Don't want to disturb him. Oh no. Oh no.

Each streamlined bird's desire is to be fat and slow. Woe woe, woe.

Did my orders come through? My 1049 to get out of the field. How else can I start my walk to Hanoi? Me. In white robes, the harbinger of peace, walking right across the DMZ with a white flag flying and white skin and the whitest heart in South Vietnam.

Montagnard women pass behind the bush, each one carrying fifty to one hundred pounds of rice in baskets they wove suspended from a bamboo pole, which they carry across their shoulders. How can they do it? Tiny four-foot women who weigh less than the rice they carry.

One hundred and seventeen degrees. Me, I cannot move. I swim within my own pool of sweat. But today is stand-down. We go to the beach to swim. Somebody up there likes me. We are down to 54 men, which is Company B. Somewhere we lost over one hundred. I will not come back to the field. I'll sleep on the beach. I'll swim to San Francisco. I SWEAR TO YOU, MERCILESS WORLD, WHEN I GET TO THE BEACH AND STARE ACROSS THE SEA TOWARD CALIFORNIA, I WILL SWIM TO SAN FRANCISCO. That would take me no more strength than to survive the death of heat. The death of dust. The death of stink. The death of thirst. The death of exhaustion. The death of cramps. Of leeches. Of poisons. Of losing friends.

Last week, I was nearly crucified. A mortar burst picked me up, so high, and dropped me down like a baby on my feet. Only one week ago. Only one week ago. You don't forget that easily. Ask someone. Ask yourself. Sit in front of the Tee Vee. Maybe, I'll die for you—on the Tee Vee. You with the six o'clock news with your supper. Why not? I'll die for you....Then you can finish your Tee Vee dinner and say, "I've seen it all. Now, I've seen it all."

Walking, walking,
No talking, talking.

Down and up, up and down. The strap on my back. It hurts like hell. Too much water today. I got six canteens and one of 'em ain't ridin' too well. But we get to a stream and me, I go floating across. Take a quick dip but don't get my ammo wet.

(the kids are singing that in their Sunday school parade)

I start thinking about tall, blonde women. But I doubt I'll marry one. I always figure on somebody fat. You know, nice. Good cook. Seventeen kids I'll have. My own little army of tykes.

Blam!

Blam!

"Oh damn!"

I'm down on my stomach faster than a rat shits and runs. I'm low-crawling on knees and elbows about a thousand miles an hour. I'm up to Jaspon. I pull alongside; we're like two cars at a stoplight. Only we're on our stomachs in the mud on a trail about five klicks northwest of LZ Fat City.

"Whadda ya think it was?"

"Booby trap."

"Who's on point?"

"Private Bailey."

"Damn."

"Shit!"

"I hate Charlie's fucking guts. I hate this whole fucked up place." That's all I do is think these thoughts. 'Course there's not a damn thing else I can do.

A pain in the back of my neck reminds me I've been holding my head up too long in this awkward way. I lower my head and the steel pot drops off and lands in a puddle with a splash. My nose is a hair's breadth above the water. I remain in this position looking at my reflection for a long time. My eyes are too close to focus. The ground and the puddle are a dark brown blur. "The color of shit." I must have spoken the thought out loud.

"Whadya say?" says Jaspon.

"Shit."

"Yeah, shit," he repeats with feeling.

"It's all shit, ain't it?" I think, but don't say.

Jaspon and I lie back behind this big mound of dirt we figure will protect us from almost anything and listen to the rounds buzzing a few feet over our heads. Heating up the air. Burning up the air. It's quite a religious experience to hear these projectiles traveling at more than a thousand feet per second, zooming that close. If you close your eyes you can picture them flying off to their bizarre destinations eventually settling down to earth, digging themselves deep into the awful gray mud, or into some bamboo tree, or into a hootch, or someone's leg or arm or neck....God, all those places are beginning to seem the same to me. All they are is paper targets. Like us. To the army we're as expendable as paper targets. To be thrown away after use.

It's what this fucking place does to you. Nothing seems to matter anymore. Nothing.

Last week we got on Tee Vee. We love Richard Holmvelt and the six o'clock news.

Each of us chucked a grenade down this spider hole. It was all on Tee Vee. I got no contract with NBC. I got no contract with the New York Yankees. But what a good throw!

Thirty million people saw my throw. But I bet not one considered there was a man down there. A gook in the spider hole. Hey Ma, I blew a man to hell down there. Wave to the camera, boys. Wave to the camera.

Now I remember. John Wayne is your hero. John Wayne is so big and tough. Oh boy. What can I say? Me, I'm tall and skinny. Rodriguez, he's too ugly. Foxy, he's got no personality. Bailey, he's dead. Jaspon, he's black. Zabriski, well, you know. Spellbinder, he's only a gangly kid. O'Sullivan, his head's too big. Armaruder, he's a killer. No John Waynes in this squad. Sorry, America. Sorry to disappoint you. I guess we don't get to see your casting man. Besides, we smell too much. He couldn't stand to talk to us. Hey, America. Send us some aftershave. Old Spice. Send us a barber and a costume gal. How about a make-up man? We even got an Indian. Don Catchahorse. A real Navajo from Arizona.

America...do you love us? Do you see what we do for you? It was your tax dollars bought us our weapons. It was your tax dollars bought us our clothes. It was your vote got me drafted, graduated to Beetle Eater. Bona fide Killer. Now just send us a letter and we'll see what we can do for you. Rape women. Eat snakes. Shoot gooks for fourteen hours straight. All for you. Just for the price of your electric bill. To keep the Tee Vee on. Maybe we'll arrange a few WIA's, if you know what I mean. Just a couple of surface wounds. A bullet that comes by real slow—that'll only graze the arm. Just like it would happen with a movie star. Nothing messy though. Nobody gets seriously killed.

Well, sorry. We got to saddle up now. Be back later with something more real. O'Sullivan says you like your movies real. Got to blow now. Blow the mountain's shit away.

This is one of the cards I carry in my wallet:

Be Alert — Stay Alive

KNOWLEDGE INSPIRES CONFIDENCE
Mines and booby traps can kill so be alert —
stay alive.
If possible, don't be in too much of a hurry.
Never take anything for granted, it might look
harmless but it might be a killer.
Evidence of old camouflage may indicate mines
and booby traps.
Suspect all objects that appear loose or out of
place.
Always look for trip wires.
Never bunch up and become a good target for
command-detonated mines.
Destroy mines and booby traps in place or
mark, report, and leave them alone.
Before cutting trip wires, check both ends for
booby traps.
Objects should not be disturbed without
checking for booby traps.
Be especially careful in areas where you are
expected to slow down, bunch up or become a
good target.
You can learn a lot from the local people, seek
their help in locating mines and booby traps.
Since there was nothing in the area yesterday,
don't assume there is nothing there today.
Mines and booby traps are favorite devices of
the VC/NVA. Grenades, spike traps, AP and
AT mines and a variety of other means are em-
ployed to harass, slow down, confuse and kill
friendly forces. The forms of these weapons are
limited only by the imagination of the designer.

Sometimes a bullet hits a rock. Sometimes a tree. Sometimes it hits me.

(the kindergartners sing this while they swing at recess)

Four days now we've been in this night laager and every night we've lost one man. One a night, it's very spooky. Except for the first night when we lost two. Charlie crawled inside our perimeter and knifed two guys right in their sleeping bags—and crawled back out and no one knew until morning. The second night, nobody slept. Snipers were harassing us. Another guy bought it. Then, last night some new guy blew his own shit away with his Claymore. He fell for one of the oldest tricks in the book. Just after nightfall, supposedly so Charlie can't see us, each position around the perimeter sets a Claymore about twenty meters out in front. The pound of C-4 plastic inside is enough to blow your shit away and most of your friends too. To set it up, for insurance, you stick a piece of tape or a band-aid on the side facing you so you can tell if Charlie has crawled up and turned it around. But by now he's on to what we do, so he sneaks up and turns the mine around and the tape so you think it's still facing out. Then he rattles the leaves in the bushes so you trigger the detonator to set it off and blow yourself away.

There's something very weird about being in the same laager for more than two nights. But four nights in a row, you can figure that even Hanoi Hanna knows our position and is broadcasting it over the radio.

None of us have slept for four nights now and I'm on watch with my eyes peering over our big berm—which feels like a big tabletop—on the far side from Catchahorse. I'm freaked out, thinking I'm seeing things in the dark but I'm more tired than freaked, so I stretch out on my back—

which is as good as saying "Goodnight." And I'm half asleep and probably snoring when from somewhere inside the infinite realm of dreamsville comes this incredible deep roar accompanied immediately after by a mental image of my head inside the mouth of a lion or tiger, like the lion tamer in the circus. The sound obviously comes from someplace very, very close—so close, in fact, that I feel the heat from the animal's breath in my left ear. I decide to sit up very slowly. Then, thinking better of it, I open my eyes very slowly to not freak whatever it is. But I don't see anything, so I roll over onto my right side with my finger on the trigger of my M16, moving the catch off safe ready to blow its shit away, whatever it is. But nothing's there. My heart is pounding and I crawl back over the top of the berm to wake Catchahorse down in the bunker under a roof of banana leaves. I crawl on top of the roof, which proves how strong we've built it during these four days. Catchahorse is awake. It happens that any three guys in a situation as freaky as this become so close they can read the other's thoughts. Especially when something spooks one of them.

I am about to say, "Did you hear that?" But I know he did by the look on his face in the moonlight. He crawls to the top of the berm and we stare out in front of us down the trail, leading out into the paddies. There, from the top, we see the thin, white body of a tiger as he hurries along the trail silently at that cosmic speed only certain animals can move at where it appears they're hardly moving at all. Neither of us says a word. Jaspon crawls up a few seconds later but he's too late. We don't tell him anything—he isn't going to believe it anyway.

The three of us stay awake now and we all take up positions out in front of the berm. A few minutes later, we're having a smoke when somebody crawls over with a radio report: an NVA regiment is expected on the trail—the one the tiger was on—coming right at us sometime in the night. Spooky, which is this airplane fitted out with radar and infrared sensing devices that flies so high you never ever hear it, has made a definite identification of unfriendly movement of about a thousand men, heading exactly in our direction—about seven klicks out. Several hours away. Maybe less.

It's hard for me to assess how I feel—compounded with so much fatigue.

Jaspon surprises Catchahorse and me, telling us that he's been carrying this little chrome derringer pistol. The three of us decide we'll leave the pistol on the floor of the bunker with five rounds in it so if there's only one of us left, he can use it on himself. None of us wants to get captured and taken prisoner.

Our positions on the berm are this: me on the right, Jaspon on the low side to the left and Catchahorse lying on his stomach spread-eagled on top. We count our full M16 magazines which number fourteen between us. It's been four days since we've been resupplied.

For the next hour we contemplate what is going to happen. None of us has ever been so sure that this is it. All the signs and weirdness of the past three nights have been warnings leading up to the end of the road. All together, we have this extremely final feeling. Surprisingly, it's nothing very emotional or even a bad feeling. It's just very flat and dry, like the desert—the kind of thing we'd always been expecting. It's maybe a little bit strange that it comes on this night, this particular one, but I keep thinking, why should it make any difference on which night the end comes? It might as well be this one. Still, that doesn't stop me from being scared, as scared as I've ever been since being in country—almost as scared as when I was coming out to the field for the first time on that first chopper ride. But that was more like a dream. That skinny old first sergeant who rode out with me and never said a word, never even smiled because I think he knew the thoughts that were speeding across my brain—like some evil spacecrafts from another solar system—the kind O'Sullivan says he sees when he's stoned. But now I've been here long enough—how long has it been? I don't even want to try to remember the time, the dates, because those are mortal measurements and I don't want to feel mortal at this moment. It's a strange and funny game you play inside your head in this place. There is just so fucking much time to always be thinking of things that you get to know the mechanics of your brain very, very intimately. And if I dwell on dates and time in-country here, right now, it will be as if I'm forcing those evil space crafts to land, to stop, to settle down in my head and keep me thinking about the little chrome gun sitting on the dirt floor inside the bunker behind the big berm. And I ask myself, with life as precious as it is, how could I ever believe I would end it with that little gun, the gun that shined brightly with the reflection of the moon when Jaspon took it out of his pocket. I ask myself this and the answer is—I just don't know.

Radio reports relayed from Brigade Tactical Operations keep coming in every half hour giving the new position of the regiment. One report is that the NVA are almost right on top of us. Then in the next report they're shifting direction as if they're going to hit us on our left flank. Noises rustle and rattle in the bush all night. But when it's nearly sunrise and the sky is dark gray and the clouds look very black but the foliage begins to take shape in our tired burning eyes and the enemy still has not made contact, one position on our right flank begins to pull off single rounds in some excruciatingly slow cadence—it reminds me of the endless drills in basic training when after awhile the feet just move in a certain, perfect automatic pace—and the firing is just as automatic—and pretty soon the whole platoon is going berserk and the three of us stand on the berm, which by now seems like it's a fourth person itself, and pull the triggers on our black deaths shooting them from the hip in the full upright John Wayne firing position—just like in the movies. And I swear to God it's true, we fire every single round we have, except for the lucky extra magazine I carry in my right pants pocket plus the five rounds in Jaspon's derringer. We shoot them all into the frigging banana leaves and bamboo leaves and elephant grass and all the fucking biological anomalies of this place without ever seeing one lousy NVA regular troop.

As the light grows into our fifth day, the CO calls on the radio and we all gather around and hear him tell the squad leader, "Yer doin' a helluva job out there and we're gonna get you out. Sit yer men down by the stream and wait for the machine."

So, the Old Man's gonna deliver us to the beach that way. "Oh, ain't he sweet. He's just a walking down the beach."

(you can hear the kids singing this in elementary school)

Chuck, chuck, chuck, chuck, mothafuck, mothafuck.... (my impression of the sound of the chopper come to deliver us to the beach)

Where we goin' anyway?

You'd think the pilot'd know. He calls in on the radio. Seems he got the wrong boys in us. Jaspon holds the end of his barrel to the pilot's neck. "Yer gonna take us to the beach or you'll be missin' dinner," he yells. "Don't much care if you got the wrong bodies here."

"Put that fucking thing down," I sez. "Leave him alone. He's the one's gotta take us there."

Up in the air again...
Ridin' high...into the sky.

On the beach,
We see a soldier water skiing.

Nobody can quite believe it. A soldier—looks like an officer—actually passes by—on water skis. Doesn't he know there's a war going on? Didn't somebody tell that cocksucking, motherfucking, asshole lieutenant?

We all want to shoot him straight out of the water.

So this is what they do in the rear.

So this is the Army's way of saying, "Hey."

Our boots are off, our weapons on the sand. Nine of us run like mad dogs right into the water to strangle that guy. And look at him wave. He thinks we just want a turn. A few circles on the sea. On his pair of water skis. Flying finish he does. Skating right up on the beach. Nine of us—tear the living shit right out of his bathing suit. The young lieutenant is stunned. But he gets some help. A couple of clerks come out to chuck their typewriters at us. As the lieutenant walks away, he yells, "Court Martial! Court Martial!!" And we say, "Fine, we'll take nine, please. Or more if you got 'em."

He knows we'd do anything to get out of the field.

Forget him.

Off with our clothes and in for a swim. Little nursies on the beach. One of them looks like a Georgia Peach.

(the kids are singing that all over the world)

They get to see us naked. But the nursies won't come over to play. "Animals," they say.

You see, they came to patch up the young lieutenant. First he goes water skiing. Then he gets laid. Not bad for a day in the life of a soldier. Big hero, him.

Yessir, fathers and mothers of America. Your boys are

spending your tax dollars right—we'll see to that for you. No waterskiing lieutenants will get by us.

We sit on the beach baking in the hundred and twenty degree sun, only it doesn't seem too bad out here in Miami. Nice cool China Sea breeze keeps our beer from boiling. We smell hot dogs and hamburgers and Vietnamese chicks. Oh, man, gonna get me one tonight....

Mountains smile for more than a mile.

I meet a girl named Ly (pronounce Lee).

That's the way it should appear. She's a dear. I knew it could happen and maybe I'll marry her someday. She's only sixteen. But I love her already and she knows it. And maybe she even loves me, too.

In a little village, Song My, with a Coca-Cola stand by the side of the road. I promise to be back in one week. Meet her on a Sunday, if I have to run all the way, steal a chopper and the pilot too. Ly, I love you. I'll take you home and your parents, too. She's quiet, young, and oh, so thin. Always has a smile and the hand of a friend. "Come with me, Ly." Oh, how I wish. "I'll be back to see you soon."

"But Warren, don't go."

I wave goodbye.

The nine of us go back to the beach to get high.

Miles of long, flat land stretch out ahead—
No cooling breeze and a too hot sun.

I respect Moun, our scout who walks point today. But I hate Armaruder because he hates children. I once saw him kick a young boy in the face. You wonder why the Vietnamese dislike us. They understand us all right. They see right through us. They know us from a thousand years ago. It was that long ago they learned what America is just now learning. They are old and wise. Armaruder kicks a kid for no reason and Moun sees him, and I too am judged by Armaruder's action. Moun says nothing. Moun is too wise. Too much war he's seen. Fifteen years in the North Vietnamese Army and now he leads us against his old friends. And I trust him. Some of the others don't. But I do. He saved Catchahorse's life. He saved him from a mortar he heard coming. Nobody but Moun heard it. Too much war has Moun had. No chance for a peaceful life for Moun. It makes me stop my other thoughts. I am here for one year, but when I go Moun will stay. Moun is here for always. He is the one that must live with this war. We come with our guns, our tanks, our fancy food and boots and helmets and Moun still wears rubber tire sandals which he'll hump the boonies in for the rest of his life—because he has to. We think, why? He no longer asks that question. For him it is the way of his life. It is all that he knows. From the year one to his forty-second year, war. War. You want to know what the word means? Don't ask me, ask him. He'll look at you with these eyes of his that don't seem to see you, even though they're staring right into your own eyes. He's looking at the real you, not the one standing there. Our eyes have seen Beverly Hills and Coney Island and the Empire State Building and read Ernest Hemingway and seen paintings by Rembrandt and Picasso, but do our eyes know how to see Moun? We see

44

him as we have seen the pages of National Geographic Magazine and watched Wide World of Sports and James Bond. We think we have seen Moun before, but we haven't. We've only seen this image we have of him looking like an aborigine in the photographs in the magazine. So we have a category to stick him in. From history books or TV, or anywhere. But Moun, he's never seen us before, and he can't look at us so simply. And yet he knows us, while we don't know him. He is the one who has lived history. But we are the ones who've complicated it, written it in books and stored it away in our memories. Moun has no memory—he hasn't the time to create one. How can a man who has faced death for every minute of forty-two years have time to ponder the abstract idea of something that for him is as concrete as his chest bone. We, particularly me, can see Moun as a hero. Not a John Wayne idiot, pretend, pussy hero but a living hero. A man who would sacrifice his life for my own. Yet Moun, though he wouldn't put it in words, sees us not as men but as the small chunks of fate that we are, living in his war. Just what he's done for all of his life. He doesn't understand our complicated way of seeing, yet he knows that our guts are manufactured in the same room in hell as his own. He hears us talk of Hollywood but he doesn't really believe there is such a place. And right here, where I am walking behind him, I know, too, there really is no such place. And that John Wayne is a myth.

No matter how hard it falls
The rain doesn't drown out the sound.

Task Force Cooksey: Detainee camp by Son Quan. 305 (latest count) women, children, and old, crippled men lie awake in a giant B-52 ten thousand pond bomb crater with no protection from the rain. They are being interrogated by the South Vietnamese Police who are the cruelest people I've ever seen. I feel better about America after seeing them in action. I even feel better about Armaruder. A rifle butt cracks against an old man's skull. He'll die because there are no bandages. He's done nothing wrong. Except to have been born as a man to be sacrificed. I dedicate the minds of all to him. He shows us exactly what man is. God help him. His lips move as he prays for death, the old man, his words growing faster and more frantic as he feels death approaching.

The monsoon is here. It is raining and it is very, very cold.

A newborn baby will die. He was born in the crater, and he will die in the crater.

We radio for food. God bless Catchahorse who screams and threatens to tear some captain apart on the other end of the radio transmission. The captain can't believe he is being talked to like this. He thinks Catchahorse is joking. So the captain cracks a joke. Catchahorse dies another death today.

The chopper can't get in with the food. Too much water in the air. We hear it circling above the clouds but it won't come down. So the people will go hungry tonight. Some of the children will starve and be buried in the crater by morning. We are there to hold a protective perimeter around the crater. We expect to get hit tonight from across the river. Already we are taking incoming fire. We are cold and hungry but we give up the little food we have. It is nothing for us to do. It is not an action of sacrifice. It is a pitiful gesture that makes none of us feel better. It makes me feel worse. Somehow we hope that it may save a life. But it's too little too late. Then I start to think, what are we saving these people for? Are we going to make them into Americans or some fucking thing? Are we going to patch them up, let their wounds heal and put them on a plane to Disneyland?

Somebody is hit in the first platoon. We hear on the radio that it is one of the Vietnamese Popular Forces who are holding the perimeter with us. The fire grows heavier as the day disappears. I do not want to stay the night in this place. Fuck. I fire a magazine back across the river. To spit some hate. The machine gun stops. I think I may have got him. What luck. Ha! What fucking luck.

In five minutes, more green tracers stream over our heads. Motherfucker. So much for luck. We all open up with this simultaneous hate for that invisible fucker in the bushes across the river. As I'm firing, I get this picture of a little fat kid about ten years old who's behind that machine gun. I'd like to ring his neck. I'd like to see Armaruder kick his face in.

Midnight: It starts raining in torrents. No incoming for about an hour. Then all of a sudden the enemy fire begins. Really heavy. I'm shaking like a dying bird or a scared dog. Spellbinder is more scared. He doesn't show it by shaking or anything but man can I feel it. Catchahorse is between us and stays calm. He's always that way. Rounds are coming right over our heads. Two or three inches it seems. We are behind nothing. Just on a piece of open ground. I think of the log over to our left. But I'm too scared to move. So we just keep flat. You can feel the bullets as they go past. I hope nobody buys it. But I feel they will. Somebody. But I can't be sure. It's very quiet except for a few babies crying down in the crater. All of a sudden, mortars. Oh God, Mortars. They're mortaring the crater. We hear the screams, then all at once in some terrifying frenzy—we, all of us, every single fucking guy in the whole perimeter—opens up his fucking hateful beautiful Black Death weapon on those despicable fucking creeps. God, I don't fucking care, all the rounds we have. More and more and more zap zap zap zap clap clap. On automatic we are firing like I've never seen without stopping, without stopping, there is never an end, just MORE MORE MORE MORE MORE it's never enough. It must be like the end of time. We use up everything and pray that the sky will rain bullets to fill up our chambers because the only way we can repay those dirty cocksuckers is to kill every last one. But it is late—too late. They only got in three, or maybe four, 82mm mortar rounds—but it is enough to do the job. They've wiped out the crater. It is what we all thought was possible but couldn't believe would actually take place. It's too dark to see what happened. The screams stop. But there are still some sounds, some voices, but can you imagine what it was like for those poor fucking helpless people inside that fucking mud hole wet crater in the pitch black night to have their babies and mothers and fathers and sisters blown to bits and feel their hot blood and not even know if they were dead or alive and not be able to help them or even fucking KNOW anything! Christ.

After a half hour, after it is too late, we get miniguns from the sky. Apache gunships. What the cruelest joke in the whole world that is—The miniguns shattering bodies across the river when IT DOESN'T EVEN FUCKING MATTER ANY MORE BECAUSE THESE PEOPLE IN THE CRATER ARE ALREADY KILLED FOREVER.

It's a black day today—
The day I watch courage walk past.

The Everly Brothers are on TV—Armed Forces Network. I am in the hospital drinking eight quarts of grape Kool-Aid every eight hours alternately sweating, freezing, sweating and wondering, does the Red Cross hostess fuck? "Hello, Doughnut Dolly!" I think, but it comes out loud— with my chin resting on my chest—as I stare down the length of a body, which appears from this angle to be five miles long. She passes in front of the TV, her red and white striped cotton dress swishing back and forth, while she delivers cups of purple Kool-Aid from a plastic pitcher to us hapless victims of malaria, pouring precisely at pussy level. Oh, I think I'm in heaven. My thoughts of her pussy are like punctuations in *Bye, Bye, Love*. Somehow I hear the song playing in my head as loud as if it were on the radio. Emptiness. Loneliness. Yeah. I think I might die. Thank you, Don and Phil.

I think of last week in the boonies. I can remember at least four or five mosquitos that bit me. I remember their bites at least. But which one was the real life motherfucker that injected me with these-freezing-chills-oh-no-just-when-I-thought-it-was-too-cold-in-here-I'm-suffocating-with-all-this-heat!

Which is it to be, hot or cold, Don or Phil?

The hospital is just off the beach. The water is blue, blue. That's the only way to describe it—blue, blue—because it's not just blue. Not only blue. It's so blue it could be a poem.

The Sea, in Chu Lai, in July
    Blue, blue
    Blue, blue

Blue,

Blue.

Had enough?

Outside my window there was a crowd of patients a while ago watching a show. Old Marty, the Sergeant Major who's in the next bed, insisted I sit up and watch. I had to obey, he joked, because he outranked me. We watched while a monkey fucked a dog.

Marty is a very friendly guy and doesn't mind that I call him Marty. Though, by regulation, of course, I'm supposed to call him Sergeant Major Jellowithski—an old Polish guy from Pennsylvania. His name reminds me of yellow whiskey.

Doc told me yesterday to be nice to him—he told me this when the Sergeant Major was out stone cold on sedatives. He's going to be a double amputee tomorrow. But the sad thing is, though he knows it himself, he just won't believe it. He pretends it isn't true. Doc said that even after the amputees lose a limb they still don't believe it. It's incredible, the human will. If Vietnam has taught me one thing, it's that the strongest thing in the world is man's will. If you want to believe something there's nothing on earth that can make you not believe. It's a wonderful thing, really, to know that believing something can make it happen. Just knowing this can save you from suffering.

Nursie gives me a newspaper to read.
Yip—pee! They're talking in Gay Pa-ree!!

Paris Peace Talks: Hippy Dippy Nguyen and Henry Kissy-my-ass-y, SQUARED OFF. No, not really 'cause the table they settled on is ROUND. It took them two fucking months to settle on ROUND!!

"I'd just like to say, Honorable Sir, that we feel that—"

"Oh yes, Sweet Jesus, I know but I'd like to suggest—"

"Thank you for your thoughts, Right and Excellent Secretary, but we would like—"

"Yes? And that would be…?"

"I'll take my coffee with cream, Magnificent and Glorious Chief Bullshitter."

"Oh yes, why not? I'll have a cup of tea."

Meanwhile, back at the ranch (the jungle), 122 Americans were killed or wounded today—on this day alone. God only knows how many dinks were killed. A thousand? Five thousand? Each one has a family up in Hanoi, or some suburb where the village will get word. Oh yes, "Nam or Pham or Phuouc or… is not coming home to help harvest the rice this year."

Or ever.

Or, fucking ev-er.

"Rice is nice, but it will have to grow without you, Son."
(the kids in elementary school in Hanoi sing this song)

Did you know the most common Vietnamese boy's name is "Phuouc?" This is the American phonetic spelling. But when you say it, it's "Fuck."

Fuck you. My son Fuck got Fucked today. An 82mm mortar blew him into little candy bits.

"Where's Fuck?"
"Take a look down at the ground."
He does. (Frowns.) "Where?"

"Right there. You're standing on him."
"Oh. That's Fuck?"
"I guess he really was Fucked."
"You mean, Phuouc'd?"
"Why yes, that's what I mean. Please pass the cream."

(nobody's singing this, but it makes it into the Herald Tribune)

**"Broken days
With nights between."**

I'm out on the doorstep of the 9th Medevac Hospital Malaria and Double Amputee Clinic watching a group of three Chinook helicopters pass over on shark patrol, flying parallel to the beach going from right to left. Seeing the Chinooks above the pure blue, blue China Sea somehow reminds me of the time when I was about nine or ten in Cape Cod. I was on vacation with my family and my father paid for us to go into a small tent to see Hitler's armored car. He paid five dollars each for us to see Hitler's car.

My mother, my little sister and I, followed Daddy into the tent where it was dark and smelled like oil and gas mixed with mold from the big tent. A few people were in front of us and we couldn't see the car right away because it was hidden by a canvas partition. But when we got around the edge we saw this big long black evil thing with a swastika painted on the door sitting behind some velvet ropes dramatically lit by spotlights. Up close it suddenly seemed really, really powerful like it could actually be this chunk of evil sitting right there, especially due to the bizarre way it was in the middle of a park in a resort town on Cape Cod. There was the smell of it. The red leather seats were all cracked and worn from where Hitler had sat. I imagined Hitler in a gray uniform sitting with his ass on the seat next to some equally evil general—two guys who killed millions of Jews for no fucking reason other than they were born Jews.

Fuck. We're all born something. Something that someone else can hate. Every single one of us is someone somebody can hate!

I didn't think these thoughts then, but I think them now. I was too young to know what evil meant although I had experienced it already. Every time you go to the playground or walk down the neighborhood street, evil is somewhere in someone's eyes, in another's heart, in another's voice. It waits like a crow in a tree or a cat under a bush ready to spring its little brand of evil.

Our family vacation was so screwed up because my father had broken his thumb and had a cast on it. We were on Cape Cod where we wanted to go swimming on the beautiful wide sandy beaches, so my father put a condom on his thumb and secured it with some rubber bands so it wouldn't come off. I remember we went into this restaurant where all the waiters were dressed up as pirates with patches over one eye and black pirate hats and torn shirts. Our waiter started laughing when he saw the condom and my father laughed along with him. But the rest of us were embarrassed. I was. My mother was. My sister was too young to know any better.

It was all fucked up.

I thought about the car all the way home. And a lot after that—for years later. There was something very disturbing about it, that my father with the condom on his finger paid five dollars for each of us to see Hitler's car.

I don't know what it all means. Except maybe now I know a little more about what real evil smells like.

Just behind the hospital hootch there is this giant rack with nine Hawk surface-to-air guided missiles perched on top. They are facing directly at my LZ up in the mountains. I wonder if I could tape a letter on the tail of one and send it up to Catchahorse and the boys?

A few hundred yards behind the missiles, long tall streams of black smoke rise up into the still blue sky. Burning shit. For Chrissakes, wherever you go in this country you're bound either to step in it or inhale it. What a wonderful country. It's true what Armaruder says about this place: it is a shit eating country!

They let me go swimming now. I've been hanging out eating cheeseburgers for two days, thumbing through a book. It's *Moby Dick*, the only book in the USO that is not a detective novel or a fuck story—and it has some lines I read again and again:

> "Vengeance on a dumb brute!" cried Starbuck, "that simply smote thee from blindest instinct! Madness! To be enraged with a dumb thing, Captain Ahab, seems blasphemous."
>
> "Hark ye yet again – the little lower layer. All visible objects, man, are but as pasteboard masks. But in each event – in the living act, the undoubted deed – there, some unknown but still reasoning thing puts forth the mouldings of its features from behind the unreasoning mask. If man will strike, strike through the mask! How can the prisoner reach outside except by thrusting through the wall? To me, the white whale is that wall, shoved near to me. Sometimes I think there's naught beyond. But 'tis enough. He tasks me; he heaps me; I see in him outrageous strength, with an inscrutable malice sinewing it. That inscrutable thing is chiefly what I hate; and be the white whale agent, or be the white whale principal, I will wreak that hate upon him. Talk not to me of blasphemy, man; I'd strike the sun if it insulted me."

Yes, that's it. That's really it.

It's Sunday—the day of lizards. I've seen three. One is so big we throw him apples and he swallows them whole. The medics call him George. I call him Moby. The wind is blowing in our direction. For a while the whole place smells like urine. Then the wind shifts a little and the place smells like shit. When the wind dies down, the ground reflects the sun like the surface of a frying pan. Fried piss and shit.

I go for a walk today. Pass more lizards, one of fantastic colors—red, yellow, gold, dayglow orange....A female? No, a male. Parading his stuff around. I walk past the incoming trainees in the training center adjacent to the Medevac Hospital. A hundred green troops listen to a staff sergeant tell them how they can survive in the boonies on bananas, coconuts, papaya, sugarcane. As I pass, he's telling them how to fashion weapons out of sticks and rocks. I just think, "good luck."

To get out of the sun I head inside a plywood shack, a small museum of stuff captured from the North Vietnamese and the Viet Cong.

The room is filled with captured weapons—I guess, to inspire new troops in some weird way. But for me, entering the place is more like wandering through a bad dream. French and U.S. and Chinese and Russian carbines and machine guns, sub-machine guns, pistols, medicine, heroin, opium, eating utensils, mortars, clothing, ammunition—a display of all the wonderful shapes of my nightmares.

But this is the clincher:

Dear Mom and Dad,

All is well with me. The missions are not too bad. I regret that I have been unable to write more often. I hope all is well at home.

Love,
Lan

This translation is taped beside a letter found on the

57

body of a dead North Vietnamese soldier. The label says he was seventeen years old. Here's another one:

Dear Family,

My missions have been successful and brother Tu has fought gallantly. Try to recruit all the young men you can from the village. We must try to preserve the country. The enemy is splitting up. I cannot send a gift so this letter must suffice. I hope that you, my family, and the village is well.

Brother Bao

I think of what went down on the Batangan.

It feels like my fever has returned, and my diarrhea, so I go to the shit hole. As soon as I get my pants down my ass is covered with flies. The shiteaters can't even wait for the stuff to drop. I return to my cot leaving the Vietnamese flies eating my shit and there on my bed is a small, square box wrapped in shopping bag paper. A tag has my name on it: Warren C. (for Charles) Jones. Inside is a note on a small sheet of girl's pink stationery with flowers and bunny rabbits printed along the top. It says:

Dear Warren,

I'm writing to you because I picked your name out of the box at the 4-H Club meeting. I feel it is an honor for me to write you so I will tell you a little something about myself. I'm fourteen years old and am in eighth grade. I live on a farm where my father raises corn and soybeans for sale. We live in Oran, Missouri which is near the Mississippi River south of St. Louis. I am tall for my age—I think I'm 5 feet 6 but I'm never sure because I'm growing so fast this year. I don't have any boyfriends but my girlfriends say I'm cute. (I'm putting a picture in the box for you.) It makes me happy to write you and to think that you are in that faraway land fighting for the good of that country. I would be very pleased if you would write—I know how busy you must be—But if you get a few minutes, please write me and send me your picture if you have one.

Love and kisses,

xxxxxxxxxxxxxxxx

Theresa Patricia Jones
(See? We have the same last name!!!)

Enclosed in the box is a toothbrush, a small travel-tube of Colgate's toothpaste, a bag of jelly beans, a green plastic soap holder with a bar of Ivory Soap, a white handkerchief, a miniature flashlight and batteries and a black plastic pocket comb. I put the comb in my shirt pocket and dump the remaining contents on Marty's bed. I lie back on the cot to reread the letter and look at the picture...

Theresa is standing with her back to a yellow clapboard house holding her hands behind her. She's dressed in a 4-H Club t-shirt. She holds her long arms behind her as if she doesn't know what to do with them because they're so long. She's squinting, but still her blue eyes are visible. Her curly blonde hair is combed back off her forehead and secured behind her ears, which are rather large but shapely. She's pretty and there's some hesitation to her smile as if somebody taking the picture had just told her to say, "cheese" and caught her before she had decided whether or not she was going to do it. There's a slight line above her nose and eyes that reveal more about her than anything; something more than the sun is making her frown. I think of writing to ask her about the frown then I think better of it. What if she gets the letter and I'm dead? I fold her picture inside the letter and drop it in the olive green metal trash bin.

This medic whose name, Donaldson, is written on the black plastic tag on his shirt, sits down to talk.

"Like to finish off a 'J' ?" he asks.

"Sure." I say, and feel stoned just thinking about it.

"It's sprinkled with opium," he smiles. "I've got a John Coltrane record—you wanna listen? It blows me a-way!"

He carries in this very cheap-looking olive green military portable record player that folds open, speaker and all. We light up the joint—one of the big local joints like Flowers sells in the ville near my LZ. In two minutes, I'm more stoned than I've ever been. I have some difficulty hearing the music. It's like my mind keeps going blank and flashing back to the war. I keep hearing Donaldson say, "Hey man, come back to the music—you're gone again!" He has no idea how far.

After a while he turns off the record player and we walk outside to look at the China Sea where some small fishing boats—sampans—are passing by.

"We could do it," he says excitedly, "I know it could be done." He's got a big grin on his face.

"What?"

"Sail away."

"Sail away? Are you kidding? Where?"

"I've been planning this for months," he says. What's scary is the look on his face says he's serious. "You wait here. I'll go get my map." He gets up from the doorstep and rushes off. As I watch, a small navy patrol boat speeds out of Chu Lai harbor to intercept the sampans. A sailor on the bow holds a carbine on the fisherman in the first boat. Soon, all three sampans are rounded up and tied to the sides of the patrol boat. Some sailors with rifles have jumped down onto the decks of the sampans and are checking the holds.

Donaldson runs up out of breath. "Look at this, man." He unfolds an old map about four feet high of the coastline of Vietnam, including the China Sea. On the far eastern edge of the map and to the south are the Philippine Islands. "My plan is to sail this way. I follow his finger along an imaginary line on the map. The line begins at the mouth of the Song Tra Bong River and extends all the way across to the Philippines.

"You must be crazy."

"You wanna go?" he smiles. "I could use the company. It's gonna be lonely out there without any John Coltrane."

My God, he's serious! He's got it all worked out.

"I know a Vietnamese down in Quang Ngai that builds sampans for the fisherman. He says he can build me one in three weeks for six hundred dollars—he won't take piasters or MPC—only US dollars."

"Jesus, what an idea!" I hear my stoned-self say, "You mean, you can buy a sampan with the sails and everything for six hundred dollars and sail it right out of the Song Tra Bong and end up in the Philippines and escape from this shit hole?"

"Why not? I've been sailing all my life in San Francisco Bay. Wind is wind, water is water—it's the same anywhere."

"Jesus!" is all I can say.

He gives me his whole plan: "I have access to C-rations and medical supplies and plenty of dope. We could stay stoned the whole trip."

"We'd have to," I say.

"I've plotted the course. Look, it'd be close to impossible to miss those Philippine Islands—they stretch halfway across the frigging China Sea." He pushes his finger over the islands and I can see they are real to him. It's like he's feeling them through his finger. "Filipinos love Americans. They would find us a place to hide."

"Shit, what an idea!" I think. But right now it's too much for me to focus on—I'm really stoned.

I look at Donaldson who's looking out at the scene unfolding in front of us. The sailors have handcuffed the Vietnamese on the deck of one sampan and have brought them aboard the patrol boat and are sitting them down on the deck. One sailor pokes his rifle into the side of a fisherman's head.

Donaldson folds up his map and he lends me a pair of fatigues and we sneak out of the clinic and head over to the enlisted men's club. He says nobody's going to miss us. Coincidentally, there's a Filipino band playing tonight. He says. "The Filipino strippers are a lot prettier than the Koreans. Shit, the Koreans are dogs!"

His sailing idea surfaces in my head. "I could supply the weapons and ammo," I tell him. "I can get all the ammo we need. But what if we meet up with a patrol boat? Do we shoot it out or surrender?"

"Shit, what the fuck difference does it make?" he says. "We do whatever turns us on. Hell, if we get caught, what're they gonna do, send us to Vietnam?"

"Right on!" I agree. As I watch the band set up, I realize how stoned I am. "That was some powerful shit."

"The finest," Donaldson smiles. "The chief surgeon has it flown in from Bangkok. I'll get us some beer. Save me a seat up front."

I get two seats in the second row but when he shows up with a pitcher I'm too stoned to drink any beer. The band is made up of five very small, thin Filipino guys. The lead singer is doing an imitation of Elvis Presley. We listen to about ten songs, which all sound the same. When they take a break, the stripper comes out. She's very cute and wearing a little red G-string with fringe that shakes when she sways her hips to some sort of Oriental music playing on a record player. Everybody's eyes are glued on her G-string. Nobody even cares when she takes off her top. Filipino girls hardly have tits anyway. The big question is whether or not she's going to take off her G-string and give us a shot at that lovely coffee colored snatch. Sometimes they do, sometimes they don't. This girl does, and fulfills all of our dreams, and even sticks a pair of eyeglasses belonging to a dumb-looking guy in the front row, right, up, her, hole! My God! They, are, right, up, there—aren't they? Some guy yells out from the back, "She's nearsighted!" But then a fight breaks out because when the dumb guy gets his glasses back he refuses to pass them around for a sniff. A big black dude tries to break a chair over the white guy's head, so it turns into a race riot. I don't know what happened to Donaldson—I never see him or his map again—but somehow I find myself alive on the floor very close to the door, with my face in a pool of beer without remembering how I got there. I must've been knocked cold and dragged across the room. Unless I flew. I crawl outside and hide behind some trees. I'd like to go back to the hospital but I'm too stoned to move. So I close my eyes and the next thing I know the sun is up and shining down on my face. I stink of beer so I go down to the beach, take off my fatigues and dive into the blue, blue sea.

R&R: The streets of Bangkok
In Mr. Kim's blue Toyota.

His car dances through puddles in the rain. The city is a blur of red and blue and yellow and green. Colored raindrops fall from the sky. A miracle of night. Hot steamy air. Streets slick as ice. Sounds and sights. Horns beeping. Girls on sidewalks parading half-naked along the street. I've hired Mr. Kim to be my driver for the week. We're on the way to a pharmacy to buy marijuana. He parks outside and he goes in with my twenty dollars while I wait in the car. He comes out with two packs of cigarettes: one Winston and the other Salem. Both strong Thai sticks, rolled into cigarettes with filters and all, and put back in the packs.

We pull up in front of a bar called California. Rolling Stones music escapes from inside. Mr. Kim and I sit in the car and share a Salem mentholated joint. We're knocked out when we finally enter the club, and suddenly we're swimming in a sea of beautiful Thai girls. The place is just getting started for the night. We're attacked by a series of weird high-pitched sounds that freak me out until I see it's just the band tuning up. A school of pretty girls is swimming around the dance floor like tropical fish in a tank. Like their feet are not touching the floor. Like they're floating.

Mr. Kim tells me each one can be had for just a few dollars. Instead of names they wear numbers on their backs like jockeys on racehorses. Weird.

He is trying to decide which one's for me. Finally he says, "Number 21 best for you." Before I can speak he catches her eye, snaps his fingers and the girl lands at our table dripping with perfume and slides into the booth beside me. She immediately puts her hand in my lap. "Buy her a drink," I hear Mr. Kim's voice somewhere in the back of my brain. But I don't like her at all, her wide lips coated with dark red, her pushed up breasts, and her skin shimmering like a fish landed on a dock that hasn't yet dried off.

"She's not the one," I tell Mr. Kim, politely, figuring the girl doesn't understand English. "I'll pick my own when I'm ready."

I drink my drink and see a girl in the back, barely of age. She's taller than the others and thin. Mr. Kim shakes his head. "No—not her. Too new," he protests. "No good for you," he objects. "She don't know," he complains, meaning she's not experienced enough. But she's just what I want. She looks like a girl I might've met at a mixer at Sarah Lawrence.

"Call her over," I order him. "Number 64." He's aggravated and doesn't agree with my decision but stands up anyway and crosses the dance floor and approaches her. I see her look over at me. When he walks her over, she's so shy she can't look up. Instead, she stares at the floor. I see her trying to smile but wanting to cry. I like her a lot and hope she will like me. We get up to dance. I'm shaky on my feet. She's as soft and as smooth as an orchid petal and smells like lime. Her name is Pensi. Or Number 64.

When I return to the table the first girl is long gone.

"Pay at the bar," Mr. Kim frowns. Pensi sits while I walk over to the bar and pay the man $40. I almost can't believe it. Two $20 bills and the pretty girl is mine for a week. Back at the table, Pensi is sitting there all unhappy and scared and twisting her long mahogany colored hair in her hands. She's the prettiest girl I've seen in a long time. Beautiful high cheekbones. Long, thin limbs with breasts that fit her shape. We dance some more and she slowly loses her shyness and I feel like I'm flying with her to someplace I've never been. I can hardly believe such a girl is mine.

"You kiss," Mr. Kim laughs, looking like the devil in disguise. "You can. You bought. You own."

Already I'm feeling protective of her and want to get her away from this place where the girls wear numbers and everything seems cheap. Mr. Kim drives us to another bar. This one is named Washington but it's just the same as the California only the band plays the Beatles instead of the Rolling Stones. The girls here wear numbers too and I'm still caught in the same dream.

Mr. Kim drives us back to the hotel.

Two American women follow us into the elevator. Obviously American military officers by the way they look and walk. But friendly enough. They have the room next to mine. We share a quick smile as we close our doors. The unspoken look we share is all about sex. It may be that we're having different kinds, but that's no matter, so long as it's sex. Sex is why we're all here.

In the room Pensi and I undress and order some drinks from the bar downstairs. Pensi lies naked on the bed on top of the sheets and doesn't bother to cover up when the waiter arrives. I still can't get it out of my head that she's mine without even being sure what that means. Do I own her, as Mr. Kim says?

I sit down on the bed and drink my drink. But mostly, I'm drinking her in. She picks up her glass and only takes a sip. Then for the first time we kiss.

Don't know who owns who, but the kiss is pure bliss. I can feel how soft and kind she is. From that one first kiss it feels like I know everything about her. I can feel her wanting to go slow. So I try.

I want to get to know her. After all, we have seven days and no place we need to go. We begin to make love like we're newlyweds on our wedding night. Pensi begins to instruct me how to make love Thai style, lying on our sides next to one another.

Each time we make love it's sweeter than the last.

I lie back on the pillow and relax for the first time in months.

It feels like the first time in years, maybe in this lifetime. It hits me what it is—it's the feeling of safety. I'm feeling perfectly safe. No fucking North Vietnamese soldier is going to break the door down and spray the room with bullets.

It seems that even the two women next door have been put there for our protection. We have corner rooms so their door is at a right angle to ours as if they are guarding us.

I lose that thought. It is gone.

As I drift off someplace with my nose against the satisfying hot-iron smell of the pillowcase, I gaze into Pensi's half closed eyes and I drop into dreamland. I feel her fragile fingers grasping my forearm and not letting go. As if I am some sort of lifeline.

Here we are, this Thai girl and I, yet she takes on the persona of many girls back home that I loved. I think of Jane and me playing tennis for the first time and how when she looked over at me I felt an immediate pang in my heart. And how I saw she felt it, too. It was that way when I first saw Priscilla, all glowing gold with her fine thin face and body and her golden skin and her golden hair neatly tucked behind her ears as if each strand of hair knew where it belonged. And then later, there was Sara in college. Sara with the most beautiful mouth and the most beautiful brown hair on the face of the earth.

As Pensi falls asleep I feel her grip loosen. My eyes open and I peek at her for just a second and I feel the same warmth that I'd felt for all the girls I'd known, as if I'd fallen in love with each one so easily because deep down they were all the same—and they were in a way. As if they each contained the same soul, the same heart, and each one was a gift given to me, even the one lying beside me now that I'd bought.

It makes no difference that we barely have any words to communicate, Pensi and I. It is better, in fact, that words do not enter into it. They would just spoil things. I realize, lying there, that words are a poor excuse for depth of feeling, which is the river flowing between us. Words are nothing more than leaves floating on the surface.

I had thought the war had shut down feeling for me. Cut it off. It had become too dangerous to feel. Yet I am aware of it again, lying next to this Thai girl, listening to her breathe. She is a gift I had never dreamed of.

Pensi makes a sound.

My eyes pop full open. I'm hyper aware. It's a foreign sound but I somehow understand it. I look at her closely. Study her skin. My eyes travel down her body to where she's pulled the white sheet over her hip. Her outstretched leg is beautiful. I think about how her tiny silk skirt fit in the palm of her hand when she took it off. No false modesty. Her body is exposed to the world—to the elements, is what I think.

Oh, God, please no!

Can it be that she owns me?

All she had to do was walk into the California bar with a number on her back. That's all it took. Maybe I'm a sucker for number 64. Maybe that's all it is. A six and a four. Equals ten. What does that mean?

What does anything mean?

I've only just met her. The craziness of the war. I'd fall in love with any woman in a small black skirt—one with long limbs and dark burnished skin and a pretty face and—

She breathes again and makes another noise. Sounds like she says, "Warren." But no, that cannot fucking be. She has heard my name barely once or twice: "Hi, my name is Warren. I'm a fuckin' G.I. A fuckin' grunt. A member of the United States of America Armed Forces. You know, a paid fucking killer. They pay me sixteen cents an hour to kill gooks."

Whoops—you're a gook too.
More numbers.
One, two, three, four—
What're we killing for?
What're we loving for?
Whatever it is, it can't last.
But I fear it will happen again.

For now, I roll over to the night table and light a joint. Close my eyes. The reality of the outside world is too harsh.

Let me just love you and you can hold my arm and we can be whatever it is we want to be to one another. And let that be what we are fighting for.
Love.
But it makes no sense to fight for love.
Love.

For now, no sense
sweet dreams—

My Love. I get high again as
Pensi reads a book in bed in a language strange to me.

When I awake later that afternoon, I smoke another joint and the world is in a playful mood. I want to see if I am strong enough to lift Pensi over my head—the way a strongman lifts a barbell. Pensi is very small and light. I push her over my head so she almost touches the ceiling. Then we start wrestling on the bed. It is fun for me because of her size. I am always the winner.

Finally I claim victory by holding up my prize by the feet. I walk her around the room this way as she screams her little high-pitched Thai screams. I think she's playing but it turns out that when I put her down she's fighting mad. I can't quite understand why—but before I know it, she pulls her suitcase from beneath the bed, packs and is gone. A very unexpected turn of events.

So here I am, my love gone, but in a strange way, I am happy to be in the quiet room alone.

But it turns out, there's not much time for being alone.

Room service arrives, a nameless Indian boy with two steaks and French fries that I'd forgotten we'd ordered.

I eat both steaks and lean back against the headboard of the bed feeling like "Big Strong American Bull" and smoke a cigarette.

Knock, knock, knock. Soft, light knocks like the shy Indian boy would make.

He's coming to clear the plates and collect another tip, I think, as I pull the sheets up to my waist. I have no clothes on. I've left the windows open—I can't get used to the air-conditioning.

"Come in, " I say. Then, "entrez," the French way.

The door opens slowly.

I feel I'm really in a movie now because the scene that

takes place is just too wonderful to be real. The scene had to be produced in Hollywood....

The door remains open a few inches—but still no one enters: A frightened pair of almond eyes appear barely perceptible in the dark hallway outside.

This gets Warren's attention:

Do come in, please!

Warren raises his voice to make sure he's heard. The door moves slowly, opening another inch or two. He gets up, wrapping the sheet around him, looking anxiously at the pair of eyes staring in.

He grabs the door handle and pulls the door open violently. Gripping the handle are a girl's beautiful fingers. Expensive gold jewelry dangles around her wrist.

The girl is pulled into the room by her hold on the door. She is dark skinned—much darker than Pensi. She has long, jet-black hair falling over one shoulder.

Warren gasps: My God, you're beautiful!

The girl looks up nervously. Her face is very close to his.

Her eyes are made up with turquoise blue makeup. She has on a black evening dress that reaches the floor with a split up one leg to her hip. The softest, prettiest dragon lady this side of Shanghai.

Warren: Who are you?

Girl: (nervously looks at him with her lips sealed)

Warren: Do you speak any English at all?

He puts his arm around her back, pulls her toward him and gives her a long, hard kiss. He closes the door behind her and walks her to the bed and sits her down. He kisses her again, passionately. He pushes her back onto the bed and begins running his hand up her stockinged leg through the slit in her skirt.

The girl struggles to extricate herself. She turns her head

71

to one side. Her bright red lipstick is smudged around the sides of her mouth.

Girl: (gasping for breath) Pensi sent me.

Warren: (sitting up straight, pulling the sheet about him again) Pensi sent you? (he retains a puzzled look for a few seconds until he understands) Ohhh, Pensi sent you! Then… then… you're a gift? (he smiles) So, she was feeling sorry for me. She didn't want me to be alone? Is that it?

Girl: (shaking her head) Can't stay.

Warren: Can't stay?

He puts his hand behind her head to kiss her again.

Girl: No, can't stay….Not possible.

Warren: (trying to kiss her as she turns her head) Not possible? You are the most beautiful thing I've ever seen and you can't stay?

Girl: You see, sold myself to another G.I.

Warren: What? But you're my gift… and I want you!

Girl: If Pensi find out, she kill me.

Warren: (in a more businesslike posture, getting a stern look in his eye) But I insist you stay.

Girl: (frightened) He waiting downstairs.

Warren: He'll wait. Take off your dress. You can leave the rest on. I want to make love with you.

They do.

The movie is over.

It has a happy ending.

She never undressed completely. I slipped the dress up over her shoulders and her long hair tumbled down over the back of my hands. When her bra fell away her breasts filled my palms with warmth and life. Together we undid her garters—she did one leg and I did the other—and I slid her panties off. She rolled her stockings down to her knees and I was inside her so quickly and it was over very quickly.

It was performed in one fluid motion. I don't remember her getting dressed—perhaps because I don't want to. But I didn't mind her leaving after it was done. It was like we'd performed some religious rite because it was something very quick and anonymous. It was very pure, very spiritual.

But I can't stop thinking of her now, making love with some GI turkey probably too shit-faced to see how beautiful she is. The girl was like a cat. So soft and luscious the way she opened her thighs. I'd never felt a place as warm as hers. It made me want to stay there, to live there forever. It was the easiest place to forget the war.

It was a place you'd want to own like a beautiful hacienda in Spain, the walls whitewashed, the sun reflecting from the white so bright it hurts your eyes.

I never knew her name.

Pensi is sleeping in the bed beside me the next morning as if she'd never left.

Maybe it was all just a dream.

Siam Hotel:
The pool.

Life is so nice, lolling (is that the word?) by the hotel pool. The familiar American smell of chlorinated water and the ripples that are not Thai ripples or Oriental ripples, but ripples that are just the same here as they are in America— as they could be anywhere in the world.

Pensi and I still have the two packs of fine Thai dope— the Winstons and Salems. So it's fun to smoke a mentho-lated Salem together in public. Pensi lolls on a lounge chair, her dark skin beautiful against the bright yellow cushion.

My towel is warm on the cement beside her. Feels warm like a womb. I listen to the songbirds and the wind blowing in the trees. I feel Pensi's hand on my back spreading suntan cream. "You get red," she says. I start laughing at something she wouldn't understand. I am reading Time magazine, so I think, "no, it's the magazine that gets read. And it's red—at least around the border."

I'm stoned.

"Thank you, Pen-si!" I tell her. Then start thinking in pigeon French, letting the dope carry me away. "Oui, oui! Pense—means to 'think' in French," or so I think—as I look at her wonderfully deep eyes, which because of their depth, pull me in. "You are a thinker, Pens—si. Pen-si, Pen-si, oui, oui. She lies on her stomach on the lounge chair, and hands me the suntan cream—Ban De Soleil. I lean over from my chair and squirt some on her back. I move my hand up her spine and something in her captures me. How very real and subtle she is—not in any way some crude object to be bought. And there I feel her shoulders and her wings and the backs of her arms, discovering for the first time that there's an angel in my room—only we're outside where she can fly away if she tries.

"Penser:" to think. Think of what you can do. Fly me around the city. "Pense," Pensi!

She turns on her side looking at me with those huge eyes. Her entire being is filled with a longing so strong I feel it touch me. I let it enter through my skin. The feeling is scary, scarier than hearing Charlie in the dark. I feel if I don't escape the look in her eye it will kill me. So I push myself up to my knees and I spread the cream on her back. Like a small cream-colored sun. Circle of cream. Crème de cirque? I make the circle wider with my fingers. Make circles around the cosmos of her skin. Then, I don't believe what I'm seeing—then, I do, because it's happening right in front of me. She pulls her bikini bottom down and pushes it all the way off her legs.

I hardly feel the stone terrace under my knees. She pulls off the top to her bathing suit and drops it on the ground.

She's completely naked and we're doing as we please. I hear a buzzing in my head blotting out every other sound. We're alone in our own protected chamber as I spread this magical cream up and down her universe of skin, spreading it across the cosmos.

Up her thighs. She turns on her side. Rolls on her stomach. Her legs fall to the sides. Then she surprises me even more: she pushes up on her knees and invites me in from behind. She's blowing my mind! I climb on her lounge chair and push myself inside her. Oh, God—ohhhhh my! Fabulous beyond compare. We're right by the pool, people passing by. Nobody bothers to notice. We're in our own private universe. We're swimming through the solar system: I'm Mars, fresh from the war. And she's Venus. Then we're flying far. Into the universe moving the stars around creating our own constellations. There's one I make just for her, the most beautiful shape in all the heavens—Pensi, made of stars.

We make love again upstairs, trying another new and different way. This time without passion. Just the soft, warm feeling of two bodies lying very, very close. I taste her long, dark hair. She tastes my short brown hair. We look into each other's eyes. We don't say much. There is not much we can say equal to what we've done.

I take a picture of us in the mirror on the dresser. We are sitting on the edge of the bed. Neither of us is smiling.

The next afternoon
On a motorcycle going nowhere.

Pensi and I pose for a picture sitting on a fancy motorcycle. We lean forward like we are ducking down under the wind speeding along a country road. Only we are not moving. The motorcycle is parked in the hotel parking lot. The engine is not running. The doorman takes the picture.

I've always thought of myself as a poet and so...
Fucking an Idol of Love is as much my business as anyone's.

Waiting for Mr. Kim—
A breath of blue.

It's like pure mountain air—the old Toyota. From outside we watch Mr. Kim behind the wheel dip his head to see us better. His voice comes through the glass. "Warren!"

"Mr. Kim," I say, as he reaches into the back, opening the door from inside. My princess steps in. Her skirt pulls up revealing her perfect legs, and more. I smile, because it's for me that she wears no panties. I smile again seeing that Mr. Kim now agrees she is the right one for me. She's a breath of fresh air, so free. Pensi slides along the smooth seat, well worn by a thousand less beautiful asses. But still blue like the water in the South China Sea.

She smells good, like spice. The city itself smells like spice today. We pass thousands of crazy drivers on the way to rent a boat in Bangkok Harbor to trip around the canals. We find a boat for rent. It's called a longtail. The outboard motor tilts up. It has a long propeller shaft the driver lifts above all the floating debris.

We slice through the thick water, cutting our way through the city's garbage. We cross the harbor and enter a canal where young kids swim and wash themselves with bars of soap. Shit floats by. Still, the river never loses its beauty. Dead flowers float by. So do rotten bananas, oranges, and apples. The driver takes us to the floating market where there is the smell of fish and squid frying on docks beside the canal. Mothers hold babies with feet dangling off the side. The boat makes waves, sweeping onto the low docks. A woman squeals, raising her hands in protest as we sail by. The boat driver laughs. Pensi turns her head away whenever I start to take her picture. Then she remembers to turn back and smile politely for the camera. I take two rolls of film before we've gone very far. Not even aiming the camera, just shooting it by pointing Pensi's way. Not focusing. Chance photography. But there are no smells captured on film so I think, "What's the use of taking pictures?" I feel like throwing the camera overboard. I don't, but ask the question of myself, "All the people who see the pictures are going to die eventually, so why bother?"

The driver, standing on a platform in back, turns the boat around. We leave the narrow market canal and head into the open harbor. On the horizon about a mile away there's a giant white building that appears to be floating on the water. As we come closer, it becomes a sparkling Buddhist temple. The huge structure is made of cement with pieces of cut glass and colorful tiles pressed into it. Reflected by the sun the colors shoot out, stabbing at the eyes—a staggering attack on the mind.

The driver delivers us to this otherworldly place. Looking up at it from our little boat riding up and down on the small waves, it is overwhelming. I wonder did Buddha design the temple knowing people would be blinded and forced to close their eyes and look for the world inside? Or did he want the walls imbedded with jewels so the temple would appear as an illusion? Maybe it's no wonder I don't believe what I'm seeing—maybe it's not real.

We climb out of the boat and buy slices of watermelon on a stick. Then follow a path around the building, which feels like a boat floating in the middle of the harbor.

I open the huge wooden door and a cloud of incense pours over us. Taking off our shoes, we enter the cool sanctuary inside, both of us overcome. A giant gold Buddha lies on his side. It reminds me of how Pensi makes love.

She bows and prays.

I am transfixed. Blown away by the deep feeling of serenity. Hundreds of monks in saffron robes prostrate on the white marble floor. They look like small lobsters crawling on the ocean floor. A sea of worshippers. A monk chants through a microphone, a scratchy voice somehow squeaks through rusted wires, emerging through ancient speakers. Cool air and the soothing fragrance of sandalwood. Every so often the door opens and a breeze brings in the smell of Bangkok harbor.

A reminder of the world outside.

As the crackling chant through the speakers continues, Pensi looks at me with tears in her eyes. "I have Buddha," she tells me.

I kiss her. Once again, I have nothing to say.

Outside, we run into a wrinkled couple with strong Australian accents. A man and wife with camera bags strapped all over them, and powdery white skin falling off their bones. They stop in front of us, blocking our way out.

I wonder at first what they are doing. What do they want? Then I see the looks on their ugly faces. They don't like the American GI with the pretty Thai girl. They might be Australian but they're no different from the bigots I met in South Carolina. I want to punch the old man. To flatten him out and spread him like peanut butter across the sidewalk. Or cut him into little pieces of the shit he is, making him, along with his wife, into "soup de canal." He wants to take a picture of us. Now I see! We're just some strange tourist attraction to him. I'm pissed but I know I must keep it together. He doesn't know how dangerous I am. That I just flew over from the killing place and could waste him in the blink of an eye. Killing comes easy when you're hungry with hate. He has no idea that I eat bigots for lunch.

Shit. My mind's playing games. I shake my head and smile. Pensi frowns. She knows why they took our picture. It's because we're "American GI with Prostitute." The woman reaches in her purse with the flabby skin on her arm practically falling off. She pulls out some coins and holds them out in front of Pensi who slaps the hand from underneath, sending the coins flying into the air. The guy turns red and wants to do something to Pensi but looks at me and thinks better of it.

I burst out laughing and we watch the couple scurry away.

Pensi killed them both.

I didn't need to do a thing.

Back on the streets
Swarms of people like flies.

Occasionally we see an American GI. What a drag that is. We stop into a club for a drink and meet an American deserter. He's a messed up looking black guy who wants to bum a cigarette. I give him three or four and he sits down to tell us his story, which is about him working as a pimp. I can feel him getting ready to hit us up for some bread. I don't feel like giving him any because what I have I'm saving for Pensi. He senses it and doesn't ask. He turns out to be a truly pathetic character, so I buy him a meal. He orders a giant hamburger and I get one too. All the meat in Bangkok tastes the same. Some sort of spice they flavor it with. Pensi gets some rice with little bits of chicken on top.

Basically he regrets going AWOL. But it's been over a year, so now he's a deserter and would be put in prison back home if he turns himself in.

We're happy to leave the bar and I buy Pensi a dress and a blouse. As we walk along a crowded sidewalk she tells me how she sees the Thai men and women looking at her with disgust. She begins to feel very low, so I stupidly offer her some money thinking it will make her feel better.

Then, I realize I'm being just like the stupid fucking Australian couple. Pensi refuses the money so I buy her a gold chain instead, which she says is better than money. The pimp at the bar will see it is a gift and won't try to take it away. And she can always sell it if she has to.

She tells me she thinks she is pregnant by me.

I don't really believe her. I know she'd like it if I married her and brought her home to America.

Back at the hotel,
Alone at the bar.

I have a drink at the hotel bar and read an American newspaper. I read about the war in Vietnam. A story about a battle in the A Shau Valley. The article gives the American body count as well as the North Vietnamese unlike the Army papers that never list the American casualties. Today's battle the Americans lost 9 dead and 43 wounded. The body count listed for the North Vietnamese was 154. I don't believe it.

Tomorrow is my last day in Bangkok. Then six more months in Vietnam. I don't want to think about it because I know I'll get depressed. So I get very drunk on beer, and soon I begin to feel like a soldier again.

I stagger out of the elevator into the hotel room. It's freezing—Pensi has the air conditioning on all the way. I start to shiver. We turn it down. Turn on the radio. Thai music. It is very beautiful. Very sad. We make love as always lying sideways on the bed. Then sleep until dark.

Nighttime. We have dinner downstairs in the hotel dining room. Some dishes with highly spiced fish. On the side are small bowls of peppers floating in water to make the fish even hotter. Pensi and I say almost nothing and avoid looking at each other.

I sit across from her, drinking cold Tiger beers, which slows down the train of thoughts in my head. I'm feeling sad to be leaving, and I feel Pensi's sadness as well. I think she might be even sadder than me.

Thinking about her,

I know I will never write to her.

Why bother? She knows no English anyway.

Maybe she knows ten words.
Across her forearm are twelve scars.
Where a GI knifed her twelve times.
I make a point not to look at her arm.

After dinner we go dancing at The Washington Bar.

There's a band of seven or eight. They play the same songs we've heard every night. Some Beatles and Stones. But finally they play some Otis Redding. They play *Sittin' on the Dock of the Bay*, and I think of the time I sat in a bar in Charleston and I get depressed.

I watch the rhythm guitarist most of the night. He never moves, just sits on a stool and leans back against the wall making beautiful music with his hands. Pensi and I dance slowly. Barefoot. When we are back sitting at our table four MPs, looking for deserters, come in. Pensi reaches under the table and puts my shoes on my feet. She pulls her skirt down toward her knees.

How could I not love her for that?

I wake up very early the next morning just as she is leaving.

We kiss once then we stop. She tries not to cry. I let her go.

I feel like shit.

About ten minutes later I take the elevator down to the lobby. I look around for her. I can feel she is there hiding somewhere, but I can't find her.

The hotel lobby seems like the saddest place on earth. Soldiers going back to war. Girls going back to the bar.

The bus for the airport stops outside.

I don't want to go but I climb onboard behind the two female officers who were in the next room. They look like they are in love. I think they never left their room for the entire week. Something I hadn't noticed until then: one of them is very beautiful.

Suddenly I'm sad that I can't bring Pensi back with me.
But I have some pictures she drew to remember her by.
And all my photographs.
I think of her as the color of love.
The largest emerald ever found.
Weighing ninety pounds.

I wonder who will buy her next
And will he love her like I did?

Back in Quang Ngai—
Leave your sanity outside.

I visit the medic. He says:
    Pull down your pants. Have you noticed a drip?
    No.
    Pull down your pants. Does it hurt when you piss?
    Yes.
    Two shots of penicillin. One for each cheek.
    Isn't love sacred anymore?

Penicillin takes care of more than the clap—
    The CO wants to see me. He promotes me to sergeant—I
get three stripes on my sleeve. Whoopie!

Two packages of Kool-Aid come in my mail.
Both grape.

Wide angle shot: Airstrikes—
F-4 Phantom jets fall screeching from the sky.

I'm on an air-assault and somehow get picked to fly on the Command and Control chopper with the Big Bird himself—Colonel, "T" for Todd, Randall of "Randall's Raider's" notoriety. He is known as the hardest of the hard-ass colonels. His brigade, the "Screamin' 33rd," is known for the most kills per man in Vietnam—and, oh yes, I am a part of it so he's my colonel too, my commanding officer, although I don't want to believe it. I might hate his guts and all he stands for but now that I'm a sergeant I have to play the game. He's asked me to ride along as an observer. To see how a war should be fought. But really, by what I'm observing, it all seems as crazy as I thought—another insane movie.

Fire up the cameras, please: Rockets shoot from Phantom jets, exploding in the trees. Heavy clouds of bright orange napalm follow. Huey helicopters fly in formation low leveling above the trees like vehicles from outer space, emerging from behind the orange sky.

The helicopters land and men jump out. The camera tracks higher and higher and the shot passes through a formation of gunships circling over the battle then rises above to where the brigade commander's helicopter hovers stationary in the sky.

Close up: T. Randall himself is seated in the open door of a Huey. He's a rigid, expressionless bastard with a wide red face. He wears an impeccably clean, starched uniform with his last name embroidered on a tag above his right shirt pocket. An emblem with a flaming bayonet is centered on the front of his flight helmet. Beneath the emblem is: "Fear no Evil." A tiny microphone presses up against his lips. A map of the operation covered in yellowed plastic and tacked to a stiff board sits on his lap. He carries a .45 caliber pistol in a leather holster on his hip.

A Lieutenant Colonel Blount and a Sergeant Major Barnell, as their nametags read, sit like gargoyles on either side of the colonel. From time to time, the brigade commander lifts a pair of binoculars and looks through them. When he lets them hang against his chest he holds a hand, palm down, six inches above the map getting a fix on where he is. His hand judges his altitude over the topographical map.

Sergeant Warren Jones sits behind the pilot, facing backward toward the colonel. It is very windy in the chopper. The sound of the engines is extremely loud. The camera tracks the colonel's eyes over the battlefield below. Tanks and men, resembling toys from the air, maneuver on the ground. Everyone in the helicopter communicates through the microphones built into their flight helmets in business-like monotones. The Colonel's radio call sign is "Raptor."

The radio squawks.

Radio: Raptor, Raptor. This is Red Breast. Request assistance. Over.

The colonel frowns.

Lieutenant Colonel Blount explains: That's Bravo Company, sir. He points out their position on the map.

Radio: We're caught in the middle of a minefield. Over.

Randall: Roger that, Red Breast. You must hold Fire Zone B—understand? Do not abandon your objective. You are to hit them hard and quick. In and out. You "roger" this? Over.

Radio: Raptor, We're taking casualties. We're in a minefield. Understand!

Colonel Randall's red face reddens even more.

Randall: Do you read me, Red Breast? Proceed. As ordered—Goddamnit! Out.

Lieutenant Colonel Blount looks, disbelieving, at Randall but keeps his mouth shut.

Again the radio squawks to life.

Radio: Raptor. This is Red Breast. Have two Wombat Indigo Alphas. Need immediate extraction. Situation critical. Over.

Randall covers his microphone. Speaks to Blount under his breath: This really fucks things up.

He uncovers the mic: Red Breast. Need more information.

He stops and shakes his head.

Red Breast: We're in a minefield, sir. Can't move. Critical we remain in place. Over.

Randall: Pull your men back. We're gonna give you an airstrike. Soften up the area. (Laughs) We'll blow the mines.

Red Breast: Negative. Cannot comply. Mines to our rear. Request immediate dust-off. Over.

Randall's head looks about ready to explode. He covers his microphone and scowls at Lieutenant Colonel Blount. Call in the air, Sergeant Major.

Sergeant Major Barnell reads the co-ordinates off the map over the radio: Raptor requests Phantom air support at 630592 sector three. Base of Hill 420.

Suddenly a Medevac helicopter with a red cross on the nose appears over the horizon slowly weaving its way toward the men on the ground.

Colonel Randall: Fuck this. Cancel that dustoff. Cancel the air, Sergeant Major. We're coming in!

He looks up at the pilot who sees him in the rearview mirror: Take us down, Jimmy. Take us down.

The colonel's chopper dives down with two apache gunships circling protectively around it.

The men on the ground form a perimeter for the chopper to land.

Colonel Randall's chopper descends quickly, flaring out above the meadow blowing back the tall grass. The blade-wash blows some men's helmets off. Two men rush forward, stooping, carrying a bandaged soldier. The men have filthy skin, with partially grown beards and torn clothing. Some with no shirts. Some have bandoliers of ammunition across their chests like Mexican banditos.

Warren jumps off the chopper and helps lift up a second man, unconscious, wrapped in a poncho. They lay him across the floor at the feet of the officers and the Sergeant Major. Just as the chopper lifts off, Warren pulls himself back in.

The bird lurches forward, dropping its nose as it gains altitude, barely making it over a line of trees at the end of the meadow. Soon they skim over treetops, small hamlets, graveyards and pockmarked ground that oddly resembles a moonscape. Then they're over the ocean and the chopper swoops low and rushes south over the breaking surf.

One of the wounded struggles to sit up, propping himself against the back of the co-pilot's seat. He closes his eyes while the man in the poncho, still unconscious on the floor, vibrates with the chopper. He's bleeding from a wound hidden somewhere inside the poncho.

His blood and mud-stained face rubs against Lieutenant Colonel Blount's gleaming spit-shined boots. When Blount notices the blood on his boot, he pulls his foot back and reaches into his pocket for an olive drab handkerchief. He wipes off his boot daintily like a little old lady. The wounded man against the seat opens his eyes and stares up blankly at Blount.

The chopper swoops over the huge division headquarters base at Chu Lai, approaching the hospital. It lands in the center of a giant red cross painted on the pavement. Hospital orderlies rush out with two litters. Warren jumps off the chopper as the skids hit the ground. He helps the wounded off and looks to get back on just as Colonel Randall holds his thumb up signaling the pilot to lift off, leaving Warren standing on the ground in the middle of the red cross.

Warren remains on the helipad watching the chopper climb into the sky. He turns and walks toward the NCO club, past bunkers, broken down tanks, bent radio antennas, and big two-and-a-half-ton trucks painted with camouflage. Behind him are fifteen-foot tall rows of beer and sodas and C-rations stacked on layers of wooden skids. Behind that, in the Chu Lai harbor, freighters sit at anchor, unloading more supplies.

Warren enters the NCO club. Inside, Vietnamese waitresses in black pajamas scurry back and forth with trays of drinks. Neatly dressed soldiers play pool and stand in front of slot machines, laughing and joking. Warren places his M16 on the bar and the bartender gives him a plastic check. He orders a beer. The men sitting at the bar look over at him, then look away. Behind him through the window, soldiers dive into a swimming pool.

FADE TO BLACK

The NCO Club in Chu Lai
At the bar, staring out at the water.

The sea is listless today.
It comes in and out...

It flows in upon the shit and spilt beer on the shore
It swallows whole fermented blood and foam.

I am inside the mouth of the Great Lion—THE SEA,
THE SEA.

All sense has disappeared.
I am dreaming—I'm under the water.
Under the water.
A fish comes by and she is my daughter....

Nighttime in Vietnam
(sounds like a song)

The way I figure it is…this place, Nam Viet, Viet Nam. Nam-phan, Ho Chi Minh Ville, the Big Crapper, Shit City…whatever you want to call it…the way I figure it, the place is possessed by evil spirits. Even the people themselves, a large part of them seem to be very similar in form and content to the billions of creeping-crawling things that choose to live here.

Why anybody would choose to live here is beyond my comprehension.

But why am I here? I've always believed we are, all of us, responsible for our own actions—so I choose to live here—at least for a year I do.

But what if I don't? What then?

I'd have to, "hang di!" Surrender!

Maybe that is the answer: surrender. The South Vietnamese soldiers are always surrendering. Once the fighting starts they realize nothing here is worth fighting for. I mean, what does the winner get? A land full of bugs and beetles and weird growing plants and poisonous snakes and diseased dogs and diseased cows and pigs and wild boars and tigers with bad breath and people with more diseases than you or I ever heard of. Plus, the winner gets a land that has been crapped on. On every damn inch. There is no place where you can walk where you're not likely to step in somebody's shit. And if by chance you don't step in shit, there are a thousand different types of mines and booby traps and pongee sticks and holes to fall into. The country was mined by the Japanese and after that the French and then the VC and then the NVA and then the U.S., and nobody has anybody else's maps and most of the maps don't even exist anymore. What the winner gets is a land full of shit and mines—and disease. It's no wonder nobody can win a war here. Who would want to?

We are, all of us here, always living with this wonderful fact: we know it is only a matter of time before we pull out of this place. We hear about the Paris Peace Talks. We hear about the anti-war movement. Hell, most of our friends back home are members of the anti-war movement. And a lot of our girlfriends and wives and mothers even! So we know it is only a matter of time. Even the President, our commander-in-chief, is talking about the end of the war. Yet we are still here and we all know men who have been flown off to Japan because they happened to walk in front of a bullet or happened upon one of the many, many stranger things that are possible. Hell, there's this bunch of grunts down in E Company who've been trying to blow away their CO's shit ever since I've been in country—and even before. It's become a joke around our LZ—and everybody all the way up to the general back at division headquarters seems to know about this vendetta but nobody bothers to stop it—not that anybody could even if they wanted to. The way it started was the CO, a Lieutenant Carlin, who was then a Major Carlin, led his company into a firefight with an entire North Vietnamese battalion. And though one of his companies, E Company, the recon company, had already lost twelve men, he ordered them to keep advancing. The major was leading his men by radio from the rear. Someone back at division headquarters was monitoring the major's radio conversation and apprised General Palsey, the division commander himself, who cut in on the radio and relieved Carlin of his command. But that did not bring back the twelve men already lost.

So, the remaining men of E Company have made it their personal duty to even the score. They plant plastic explosive under the lieutenant's bunk, under his desk, under his chair, in his crapper even. But so far they haven't blown up the ellusive bastard. Nobody ever knows where he sleeps from one night to the next. Maybe he doesn't sleep at all....

The rest of us wait for the explosion almost every night inside the LZ but even when we hear a blast we figure they've missed Lieutenant Carlin again. Some assholes just can't be killed.

And while such craziness goes on, we aren't sure that we care if we win this war. Maybe—deep down—we don't even want to win!

Win what?

Dog shit.

Water buffalo shit.

Pig shit.

Snake shit.

Bug shit.

Ant shit.

Human shit.

Jaspon, the great Vietnamese War scholar, concludes: "Sheeeeit Boss! That about sums it up—don't she now, Boss?"

I admit this analysis doesn't go deep. But when you consider it, it need only go as deep as the shit spread like peanut butter across the surface of this land.

About the only thing I think worth returning home with is a Vietnamese girl. And they are bound to have a variety of diseases, and no matter how pretty they are, they turn into old ladies too soon and start chewing betel nut which gives them rotten purple mouths by the time they're twenty-one. And even they are full of shit, if you think about it.

Am I being hard? I am. This is a hard place.

I'm just trying to keep my sanity and I am just telling you what I see.

I see: Two-ton armored personnel carriers, eight-ton amphibious ducks, twenty-two ton mammoth tanks, gigantic C-141 airplanes, Flying Boxcars, B-52's for Chrissake—all these things together with rows and rows of infantry soldiers, battleships, amphibious landing crafts—brigades, battalions, divisions, regiments, the whole God-forsaken Army, Air Force, Marines, Navy, Coast Guard—and even the Doughnut Dollies who sometimes serve hotdogs too—we are all of us marching, dive-bombing, crawling, humping, rendezvousing, reconnoitering, attacking, the biggest Goddamn Shithole that anybody's ever seen. Yes, that's right, Mom, the troops are gathering, moving out, moving into their infinitely dark black abyss—the one and only Cosmic Asshole. And what's going to happen is the biggest cosmic crap of all craps, right here twenty kilometers west of Quang Ngai City. You may not believe it, but I've seen all this with my own eyes, Babe. And I'm ready for the final blast when it happens. Not only the one that takes out the ex major but the one that takes out the country.

We fight with Kelvinator machine guns, Frigidaire rocket launchers and General Motors tanks. We Americans, the greatest manufacturers on earth, know how to equip our troops.

You should see those Chemical Platoon guys. They get up real early in the morning with such looks of excitement in their eyes, loading these great big 55-gallon drums of the most poisonous witches' brew on earth onto helicopters and fly around like Santa Claus with Christmas toys, opening them, opening them, opening them, dropping tons and tons of green powder, yellow powder, orange powder, bright red dayglow powder...

Somebody American had to pick these colors. But nobody really knows what this fucking stuff is. All the chemical platoon guys know is what the stenciled codes of death on the cans tell them: The Green powder defoliates. The yellow kills flying and crawling things. The red powder kills humans, and the orange powder, well…nobody's quite sure what that does.

It's like the chemical guys went out in their station wagons and bought the stuff at Sears. I swear to God, they must have….

You've gotta love this war—it's got the same unreal feeling as I imagine the Las Vegas strip has at 4 A.M.

So the question becomes, "What is the karma of these people—of this place that has always been, that is now being, invaded by other people from other places?

The DA—No. 550-55 Area Handbook for South Vietnam says that the overthrow of the Kingdom of Nam Viet happened first in 111 B.C.—by the armies of the Chinese Han Dynasty.

Then, there was the Din Dynasty (968-980)
The Ly Dynasty (1009-1225)
How about the Tran Dynasty? (1225-1400)
The Chinese Interregnum (1406-28)
And the Le Dynasty (1428-1788)
The Tay Son Uprising (1776—that's a
coincidence!—1802)
The French Conquest (1858-83)
The Japanese Occupation (1940-45)
Then the Communist Movement. I learn that Nguyen
Ai Quoc is Ho Chi Minh's real name…not quite as cool,
is it, Uncle Ho?
Then comes the return of France.
The Indochina War (1946-54)
Then us.
How long before the next war?

O'Sullivan, Jaspon and I talk about the leaders who run

our American war. I usually have the most vivid of mental pictures of these people. Lying on my back, hands under my head, gazing at the swirling sky, I say, "I see General Palsey. Got him yet?" I ask.

"Christ, Jones. I got him in full color," O'Sullivan replies.

I go on. "He's got rows of buttons down his front, rows of metal and brass, and the prettiest colored ribbons and birds that look like doves with arrows in their beaks and tuna fish with rifles and elephants shooting mortars out their trunks and lions and tigers on his shoulders eating each other and little kids hanging from his pockets, brothers and sisters with knives, cutting each others' guts out and he's got stars all over the place flashing like neon, on and off, and crowds of screaming people and planes flying in circles above his head wherever he walks and lines and lines of troops marching in cadence behind him and on the sides of him and underneath him and everywhere just shooting at everything that moves and battleships in the puddles he walks through sinking enemy ships and every time he comes up to a beautiful girl he lifts his arm and points with his platinum bejeweled swagger stick and four volleys of tracers splash through the girl's skin while the general smirks and cleans his teeth with a gold toothpick."

"Yeah," says Jaspon.

"Yeah...let's light another joint," says O'Sullivan softly. "I see him all over the place!"

Guard duty
Advance, be recognized.

Halt.
Who goes there?
Advance.
Who goes there?
Step front.
Forward.
Be recognized.
Backward.
Halt.

Be recognized.

Press drops of water between your palms
Hear silence scream.

I sat on top of a mountain last night separating out human light from darkness. I was cold but first I was afraid. Having survived crashes of shells and whistling of quick bullet's wings I was shocked at my being—afraid. I'm a sergeant now. And I've been here long enough that that shouldn't happen.

March. April. May.

I know I'm beginning to lose it. My mind's taking trips on helicopters that don't exist. Helicopters that fly much farther than the borders of this thin country. Imaginary borders. I've never seen one single draftsman on the ground. There are no red lines like on maps weaving between jungle trees going from north to south in the evening breeze, creating an illusory picture of a place that does not exist in reality. Really, there is no such place as Vietnam. It's as if somebody, something, some collective consciousness down through the ages needed a place for terrible things to happen. For young, healthy, strong young American boys to spend a year to be tested in ways they never could have imagined where at any moment their minds and their bodies could be blown into fragments that disappear and are forgotten in an endless jungle. That's what I'm doing here in this imaginary version of hell.

Yet there really is no such thing as hell.

It's only something we create out of fear.

And, yes, I admit, I'm afraid. So I'm here. I've willingly entered the gates of hell.

It's so hot here. Beyond what a man can stand. It fries your brain so that your thoughts cease to make sense. Your thoughts haunt you in the night. Deep, dark, horrible, frightening visions of things that have happened mixed with things that may happen, that will happen.

Dear America, the neurotic.
Dear America, the beautiful.

Soft summer night.
The top is down on my Austin Healy.

(this is a dream)

Priscilla laughs like a madwoman. She holds my hand.
We drive four hundred miles an hour along a narrow road
in New York State. We don't know where we are going and
don't care.

No sense of time.
Or place.
Screwed up mess.
Beautiful moon.
The sky is a giant circus tent.

I am some sort of ringleader to myself.

(this is not a dream)

I walk across the hard dirt of Landing Zone Zebra with
a .45 clapping against my hip. I am hip. I am tall. Man, I
am right. I feel like Matt Dillon tonight.

The sky is a silver movie screen.
I am some cowboy hero.

I stop to light a cigarette.
But it turns out to be a joint.

Somebody like the Rolling Stones
Plays music in my head.

It's a very crystal kind of reality. Too clear and crystal
to be seen by millions. A few voices filter out of some tin
huts. Fly around the air like moths in opium smoke. It is
very dark. Charlie may decide to do something. I don't
care. I couldn't give a shit. I am too cool. I feeeeeel the
sounds of my boot bottoms on the hard dirt. I am alone. I
could not be more alone.

I reach up into the sky, which is thick like molasses. I
stick my finger in and move the stars around. Using my
thumb and forefinger I flick the Southern Cross and make
it sail across the sky.
Oh my.
Oh mmmmyyyyyyyyyy.
You don't get many chances like this.
When you get one, you've got to take it.
Don't let it go. Live with it for a while.
It does you good. Lets you learn.

The picnic is never over until someone throws away the
bone from the last piece of fried chicken.

If you want to think of war: Think of chopping off
your arm or foot. Think of chopping off your thoughts.

You don't need to go insane—
Just let your heart go mad.

War is a heavy place for you to exist in.
But you will survive: the mind never allows itself to
imagine more than it can handle. The mind never knows
more than it can understand.

War fills us to the brim.
Only death overflows.

Put incidents on a page.
Read braille with garageman's fingers.

Sara writes me a letter.
She starts with, "Hi!"
I can't read any more.

It's Lou Gehrig's birthday today.
I shit you not.

Hump.

The fan swirls.
The kingdom falls.
The king goes off to study for a year at Harvard.
He used the bone in his finger for cleaning his nose.

It is getting hard for me.
Please try to understand.

When you can dance a dance without moving…
come to me.

Only when you know—who Bouncing Betty is…
can you go on reading this.

What wonderful news:
Fuck you again Vietnam.

I'm returning from three days in Chu Lai where I took a course for sergeants. "How to be a Leader of Men."

I'm on this Big Screaming Chinook which makes so much noise it feels like the inside of a nightmare—and we fly very high for a helicopter, getting way, way up because, oh shit—here we go again—we're going into the mountains which are just so Goddamn frightening every time you fly out there—and I don't care how many times you do it, it never changes. It's all gray and cloudy this morning and LZ Zebra has been under siege for three weeks and already six—yes six—birds have been shot down. They say it looks like a stateside junkyard down there and, shit yeah, it does. The machine gunner who sits in the big open door in the tail of the Chinook motions for us to look down and we do and see a chopper just like the one we're riding in, three thousand feet below us, lying very peacefully on its side. It looks like a baby sleeping. Our chopper circles round and round, first counter-clockwise and then clockwise and it feels like some Indian dance of death—are we gonna end up on our side? And I start thinking, as I always do when I've been away for more than one day, who is going to be left in the squad, in the platoon, in the company when I get back? And the names start flashing across my mind: Spellbinder, Catchahorse, O'Sullivan, Rodriguez, Castress, Zabriski, Jaspon, and of course Armaruder—and I try to stop the march of names but they won't stop so I just let them march on past until they're all gone by like some parade in an old newsreel.

The gunner gets an order in his headset and soon he's thumping away on the big 50-Cal bolted down on the big flat tailgate. And it becomes a very weird scene because I'm sitting on top of hundreds of crates of ammo and C-rations and don't have a clear view of what's going on. From where I sit, there is the peaceful panorama of the lush, green mountains. Can't see any signs of war or shooting going on—no smoke, no burnt-away hills—just peace and serenity. But right in the foreground is this gunner going manic, starting with the 50 until the barrel gets too hot and starts glowing red. Then he scrambles back, grabs an M60 and sits way out at the end of the tailgate and continues going manic. The chopper makes another circle and finally I see what is happening. The ground is covered with bursts of smoke—enemy machine gun smoke coming from the hill just a couple of hundred meters from our old friendly LZ. Charlie's going nuts. This corporal sitting beside me motions to the side of the chopper. I see light through the holes in the thin metal skin. Oh shit. The chopper dives toward the LZ, racing to just-get-the-fuck-down-out-of-the-sky so we scream on in and thump down hard and the gunner moves and yells at the top of his hyper-breath to help shove the ammo and chow crates off. So, we do and five or six more guys come running over and the first one I see is Don Catchahorse and then Jaspon and I get tears in my eyes I can't hide and the three of us embrace like a bunch of sorority sisters or some Goddamn thing—and now I know I'm back. The three of us steal a crate of chow and a sundry pack and find a place to sit behind a pile of sandbags. We open cans of the pound cake I rode in on and two of them have lead bullets inside.

"Sheeit, man," yells Catchahorse. "The pound cake saved your skinny ass!"

They are acting real light and talking some shit, but I can see in their eyes, especially the blood red eyes of Jaspon, that it's been a bad few days. They tell me seven men were killed when the LZ was overrun a few nights before. And there is this death list Jaspon and Catchahorse read off from inside their brains and it is clear to all of us that they almost say the same names at the same time. When they are done, it is difficult to find anything more to talk about—but I realize one thing: that these two guys are the two best friends I ever had. We all realize it. The whole thing is a déjà vu because, back up there on the chopper, I'd read out the same list to myself in exactly the same order—only I'd read the live guys first, they being somehow closer to the front of my mind. I don't know what part of my mind is sectioned off for the dead. What I do know is that it's in the part that wants to forget.

The whole scene is unreal. Later, when Catchahorse shows me the heads of the dead NVA that were cut off and put on the stakes supporting the concertina wire around the perimeter, I have some feeling for what happened. For days, I get told more and more stories until the stories melt into my own experiences and the two become almost like I was there.

We have our hill and across the valley with all the dead helicopters, they have theirs, with the NVA flag flying and bunkers dug in and all. To me, it is the closest thing to what it must have been like in the Civil War where the Union soldiers and the Confederates could see each other's faces.

We have called in so many airstrikes and have lobbed over so many artillery shells and 106 mortars on their hill that only one tree is left standing. Everybody feels sorry for that tree—it has made it through all those explosives—so we want to let it stand. And we all hope it will. I think about how frightening all the shelling must be for the trees and how they must be scared shitless from what we do. I never thought about it before, about all the animals we must kill—and even the creepy-crawly things that get fried in this war.

But the next morning when we awake—it has become a ritual to check out the tree—the wind has blown it over. It lies on the ground on its side and reminds me of the reclining Buddha. Only it looks more like a dead soldier that would've been made into a bronze statue after a battle in Okinawa or some fucking place in the Second World War. After that, as superstitious as we all are, nobody wants to be on that LZ.

In a few days, we have orders to move out.

La, la, la—we're flying to La-la Land!
(hell, *everybody's* singing this tune)

My squad and I are rattling around in a chopper over Indian Country. The Chinook skims the treetops floating up and down with the grace of a ballerina before dropping down quickly into an open meadow. There's a perimeter set up with some grunts hunched over their M16's with a couple of 50-Cals facing into the tree line on two sides. From the air it looks like a typical raggedy-ass camp with nothing out of the ordinary. But touching the ground, the place feels creepy—Creepy with a capital C. GIs drift around doing the usual—cleaning weapons, boiling C-rats with heat tabs and chunks of C-4 plastic. But there's unmistakable tension and weirdness in the air.

I'm appointed squad leader for the mission we're on, but so far nobody's told me anything. Back on Zebra all the first sergeant had said through his broad smile half-hidden by his red mustache, "Your mission is Top Secret. That means you and your men will leave your ID's behind. No dog tags. No wallets with driver's licenses and pictures of your girlfriend." He chuckles. "Don't matter anyhow—your best friend's with her now. Carry nothing on your person to identify you as an American soldier."

Shit. I've always had a problem with that phrase, "on your person," which makes it sound like the person he's referring to is someone else, some other me. Maybe even someone who's already dead.

And like, does anybody think I'm going to forget I'm an American Soldier when I'm dressed all in fucking olive green, for Chrissakes, and been trained for six months how to kill somebody thirteen different ways. Just in case I forget, he hands me a jar of olive green paste to cover our faces.

All I know is we've landed three shits from nowhere. We're so far into the boonies we can't smell a single village or see a single rice paddy. Other than the guys in the camp and us, there are no signs of human life. Judging from the length of the chopper ride, we are 25 or 30 kilometers into the bush. Deep into pink territory and very close to Laos. High above the mountains to the west, where it's a good bet we'll be going, we all see huge clouds building up like skyscrapers in the sky.

It seems like the guys here know something we don't. Like they know we're being sent on the kind of mission we might not return from. This would explain their uncommon politeness. Whenever I make eye contact, there's nothing but smiles for miles. We'll know we're goners for sure if they offer us a last supper. But when Cookie clangs a pot in the mess tent it's breakfast as usual— "shit on a shingle," corned beef on toast made with some kind of nameless meat that could've once been any living thing.

After breakfast a tall, skinny first lieutenant with ash black hair and Winker written on his nametag greets me like I might bite. He summons me and Sergeant Armaruder, who's second in command, to meet the CO, a Major Duckworth or Fuckworth or something.

We find the major in a tent with a map spread on the ground. Surprisingly, he looks like he's got his shit together. Then, I see in his eyes that something is missing or maybe it's something that's there. Excitement. Too much excitement at seeing us like a fox seeing a hare. He stands up to greet us when we come in. He's tall and in shape and offers us a handshake instead of a salute. Unlike a lot of officers from the rear, he knows enough not to salute in the field. The major's shoulder patch has a pair of crossed keys with a lightning bolt running between the key blades. It's one I've never seen before. It's slightly strange and somehow very powerful. I mean to ask him what it stands for but never get around to it.

He kneels down on one side of the map, with a first lieutenant on each side kneeling in unison. The cardinal with his two altar boys. Armaruder and I do our kneeling on the other side of the map. The first thing I see is a red pencil line the major has drawn following a stream from near our present location to where it originates in the mountains. Close to its source the contour lines are so close together they're almost touching, which means the land rises almost straight up.

Right off, Major Duckworth tells us in a matter of fact voice that doesn't betray an ounce of the excitement in his eyes that we will be paying a visit to the Ho Chi Minh Trail. He doesn't need to tell us what that is; it's common knowledge that the trail is the main supply route from North to South Vietnam and is undoubtedly the North Vietnamese Army's most prized possession. The trail itself isn't printed on the map, but he has drawn in its path with a red pencil. The border to Laos is on the map and the red line shows the trail is across the border. This explains the "no ID" part. We're not at war with Laos, so we can't be there. If we get caught, we never were.

The major makes a dot with the red pencil, then works on it for a while to make it bigger in case we might miss it.

"This is your objective. In a minute I'm going to give you the what-for."

After a short introductory talk about the value of surveillance in pinpointing the size and location of enemy movement, the major explains that our mission is to plant a listening device—some new secret gizmo that sends a signal back to Chu Lai when there's enemy movement along the trail. He looks my way for a second and assures me it picks up the subtlest vibration. I flash on Priscilla's roommate

113

Sara for a second and her subtle sexual vibration.

It isn't my job to question the reason for a mission no matter how lame I think it is. I'm just a sergeant; he's a major. He undoubtedly gets his orders from a colonel or a general. Besides, just in case we don't take him seriously, he's got two candy-ass lieutenants beside him just to kiss his ass on command and do his dirty work.

And one of them does when Duckworth says, "Give me the co-ordinates, Lieutenant," so Lieutenant Winker reads them off a piece of paper and the major copies them on the map under the dot. Then the major turns and sends a look at the other lieutenant who's blonde and a little too fat for his own good to be in the field. So Blondie snaps-to and understands it's time for him to reveal the "what-for." He reaches for a box that's been strategically hidden behind his feet and starts to hand it to the major who extends his hand to stop him.

"Remove the device from the box, Lieutenant," the major barks.

When Blondie fumbles with the box but can't seem to get it open, he looks just like one of those clueless bimbos on a TV game show trying to unwrap a prize. I can almost hear the laughter from the audience.

I take advantage of the moment and say, "Maybe you should have the lieutenant plant the device, sir. We'd be happy to have him ride along."

Armaruder looks at me like he's actually proud.

The major smiles too. "That's funny, Sergeant but I'm confident you'll do a better job than the lieutenant here."

The lieutenant scowls. Finally, he gets the cardboard box open and pulls out an eight-inch square plastic box that's colored olive drab with black codes written all over it. A single word that catches my eye is "surveillance." I think, what about the surveillance aircraft that's supposed to be doing the surveilling? Isn't that what Spooky does—surveil?

The lieutenant hands me the device and the major says, "Good luck" And shakes our hands. "Your orders are to bury the device at the specified co-ordinates. The instructions for deployment are written on the bottom," he smiles proudly, as if the designers had thought of everything. Like putting the instructions on a jar of instant coffee: "Stir rapidly. Add milk and sugar to taste."

Then he adds, "I'm counting on you, Sergeant Jones," he goes on, "The Army is counting on you." I expect him to say, "Your country is counting on you," or "the whole fucking universe is," and wonder why he doesn't.

"Wait one!" The fat blonde lieutenant pulls on an end of something that was also in the box and expands it to about 3 feet. It looks like a car radio antenna. It's painted olive green to match the device. "The antenna easily attaches to the top. It screws in. Exact instructions for deployment are written on the bottom."

Yes, we know.

They're all smiles until I stuff the box into my pack like it's just another carton of C-rats, neglecting to give it the proper show of reverence. The box is surprisingly heavy with that well-made feel, like it's manufactured by some big-deal company like Raytheon that makes radar and Hawk missiles.

Armaruder and I are happy to take our leave from Major Fuckworth and his ass-kissing sycophants.

We gather up the squad. No time to think—
No time to worry, No need to pray. Time to go.

Before we know it, we're humping our way to Laos. Our stomachs are full. Like we're fattened up to die. But for now we're on a tour through the countryside. The scenery is exquisite. No smell of shit out here. If I didn't know where we were, I could almost feel happy.

Loom soon,
You big monsoon.

It's an easy hike along the stream. As we hump along its bank there's a lot of time to think. I'm trying to keep my thoughts in the present and not obsess about where we're going. The weather helps with this when the clouds belch a few times and the ceiling collapses. We're in a deluge, and the rain is so hard and fast, it hurts when it hits. In seconds we're soaked through to our underwear.

I'm trying to think how to make my underwear not wet, to think how to make my socks not wet. To think how to make the water from the hood of my poncho not slip around my neck and drip down my back, and send chills up my spine.

Fuck thinking!

Thinking is overrated. I'm prepared to surrender my mind. It's been overused.

(but it won't stop)

Water drips from leaves. Water bounces off trees. Water splashes in my face. My skin is shriveled up like I'm 90. The rain makes me old. My boots go "squish, squish," with each step. I've got to get them off and dry my feet by a fire. Fire?

(my thoughts depart the present)

I think, what fire? Some sort of sick joke? Can't do anything Charlie might see. I wonder, is this monsoon falling on Charlie too?

(my thoughts enter fantasyland)

I doubt that Charlie's being rained on. He's probably nice and dry, sitting in front of the Tee Vee, watching The Late Night Movie: "Road to Hanoi" with Bob Hope and Bing Crosby and Dorothy Lamour and Veronica Lake and Myrna Loy and Eddie Cantor and Joan Crawford and

117

Priscilla Lane and John Payne and the Korean tailor back at the PX in Chu Lai.

God, I pray that I don't get the rot too bad. I've heard of guys getting it in the crotch. Man, do, I, think, this, place, sucks.

Whatever happened to bliss?

We camp overnight—
Nobody roasts marshmallows.

A day spent humping the major's pencil line and we're nearly at the foot of the mountains. Close in, they are much taller than the story the map tells. At least the rain has stopped, but everything, including us, remains wet. The water makes the grass slippery as ice, so it's good we don't begin the climb until tomorrow.

I pull my pant leg up and feel a leech that's grown fat on my blood. He's hooked a ride behind my knee and is hard and the size of a marble. I fight the thought to search my body for more and decide to just let them drink if they will. But I pat the wet grass I'm about to sleep on in search of more leeches. I see one crawling on the ground and spray a stream of insect repellent onto its tiny body as it inches toward me. Contentedly, I watch him hump his back up once slowly and then relax back down as if he'd just performed miniature push-ups. I wait for it to go stiff and die, then pull the soggy collar of my shirt tight around my neck, securing it with the button under my chin. I know there's really nothing I can do. There are endless numbers of them and only one of me.

Waiting for dark, the hours pass like clouds, barely moving.

After four hours awake on guard, I crawl back to my patch of wet grass like a leech and fall asleep. It seems like I'd just shut my eyes when a few seconds later I have to open them. A hint of light erases the dark. It's 0530 hours. Another day.

Armaruder holds the map.

The rest of us huddle around him like family members. Our eyes follow his stubby index finger—the one with the black line of dirt under the fingernail—tracing an imaginary line from the laager. We've gone about 25 klicks but we still have three more to go before we start to climb in earnest and get to the colonel's red dot.

"You'll need this," Armaruder says, peering into my eyes and handing me the map. He says sarcastically, "The major entrusted you with the device. So you should take us the rest of the way."

We move for an hour through a forest of trees that grow taller the farther in we go. A double canopy above makes it almost dark. Although it's still morning it seems like late afternoon when we reach the base of the cliff leading up to the trail.

This whole place is so far off the eerie scale we hardly talk. Because our thoughts can't make sense of the place our words would just be so much blabber. Everything, including the cliff, is monstrous and out of a normal sense of scale. It's like being in some sort of mystery garden created by a Hollywood set designer. The trees are so tall you can't see the tops. Some of the leaves are bigger than we are and it makes you guess at the size of the bugs that live here.

The solid rock wall we face is 30 meters tall and so steep the jungle can't get a hold. According to the map there is no way around. Looking straight up only a few bushes and small trees cling to the rock wall. A film of water cascades down the middle of the gray rock looking like a sheer nightgown clinging to a dead body.

We pause at the base to drink. Each of us started out in the morning with four two-quart canteens filled to the brim, and mine are all empty. Nobody has stopped to piss. We fill our canteens by holding them against the rock. The smell of the cool water is of moss and rock, and tastes better than champagne.

Dunking into the stream at the base of the cliff, we begin our climb. The first fifty feet we find plenty of ledges, cracks and trees to hold onto, but after that, and especially close to the top, we are forced to stand on each other's shoulders to find handholds. Armaruder makes it to the top first and drops his arm over the edge to pull me up. I wedge the toe of my boot into a crack and grab his hand. He pulls and I push upward kicking my legs like a bug until my chin makes it over the edge. He grabs the back of my shirt and drags me onto flat ground. We pull Spellbinder up, carrying the heavy radio on his back. The three of us pull everyone else up. Once the whole squad is on top we spread out into the jungle and take up positions and rest. The leaf cover is so thick I study the map with my flashlight trying to determine where we are relative to the red dot. Miraculously, we have arrived at almost the exact spot.

Along the way here my fantasy vision of the Ho Chi Minh Trail attained cartoon dimensions. I pictured a wide-open thoroughfare with a convoy of huge Russian-built trucks with big red stars on the doors lumbering along one after the other carrying freshly uniformed NVA soldiers whistling patriotic songs.

The reality is different. Although we haven't seen the actual trail, according to the map and my calculations we're only yards away and the place is anything but a cartoon. Because of the huge trees and thick vine wrapped bushes, we can't see more than an arm's length in front of us. The air is so dense and humid that breathing is like inhaling inside a bag of peat moss. Within minutes our fatigues are soaked from leeches that have sucked our blood.

I can sense the trail. Strings of light poking through the foliage reveals a void beyond.

I don't want to waste time. We all want to get away from Charlie's house as quickly as possible. I dig a hole with my entrenching tool while Spellbinder, without reading the instructions, attaches the antenna to the device. We bury it under a few shovelfuls of moist earth. For a moment, a few of the others gather around and stare while I extend the antenna out all the way. We feel really stupid because we sort of all feel a little proud. Mission accomplished. Job well done. Major Fuckworth and the United States Army thanks us. And, I'm certain, so does the entire universe.

Doing his crazy caterpillar walk balancing on his fingers and toes, Rodriguez emerges from the foliage. He forgets to slow down or can't see in the darkness and crashes into me, then brings his face up to within six inches of mine. The look in his eyes says something is very wrong. His voice bubbles up, "Sarge, there's movement out front. Across the trail." He smiles a nervous smile then finishes. "It...it's right there." He points with his nose. Then, to make certain I believe him, he says, "Castress hears it too." Rodriguez hangs so close I can hear his heart beating. But suddenly he turns and he's gone, disappearing through the leaves as quickly as he appeared.

I lift my weapon off the ground and hold it close like a newborn baby, my thumb flipping it off safe, my index finger held ever so lightly against the trigger, waiting. Waiting for the slightest sound. The sound of a stick breaking. A rustle in the dried leaves.

Then like the devil's landed on my shoulder, everything slowly unfolds.

Two cracks, undeniably from an AK-47, come from above us. Then a third and fourth which creates the picture of a hill beyond the trail. A spitting sound follows a bright green tracer round ripping the leaves above Spellbinder and me. Another single crack comes from the right.

A bunch of them are out there.

They're shooting in the dark, so they think we're here but don't know for sure.

I reach out for the radio handset and my hand bumps into Spellbinder. Another round buries itself in the leaves. We are both flat on the ground. We can't get any lower than we already are. I pull my face from the leaves and my voice breaks out, gurgling in my throat. "Call the major for air support—I'm gonna check on the others—stay put." Three thoughts in one.

"They'll be okay," Spellbinder says, looking like a scared cat, not wanting me to leave him alone.

"Find Zabriski and stay with him. Call and get us a fucking gunship."

"They'll want the order to come from you, Sarge."

"Say you're me." I see a frown so I assure him. "They won't know the difference."

I head off on my stomach and bump into Jaspon. He sits still as a rock, facing down the edge of the ridge. I grab his shirt to turn him around. His role is always to protect our backs. "No threat from down there," I say, and he agrees.

He grasps my arm in his huge hand and squeezes. He's calm and steady under fire. In a way, Jaspon is the best of us. We hear someone crawling from the direction of the trail. We lift our weapons and aim in unison. Catchahorse appears through a narrow alleyway between the bushes. A grateful shudder runs up my spine.

He says softly, "Charlie's right in front of us—thirty meters up and out to the right, above O'Sullivan and Sergeant Armaruder."

I tell him, "I'm gonna check on Castress and Rodriguez," because I'm worried they're going to start shooting.

"They're way at the end, past Sergeant Armaruder."

I pass behind O'Sullivan and Armaruder and in about 15 meters find Castress, our newest body, huddled in the bushes with Rodriguez.

I can just barely see Castress stuffed inside the leaves, sitting with his weapon propped in his hand. Daniel Boone waiting for Indians.

"What's kick'n, Sarge?" Castress nervously says and much too loud.

"Shut the fuck up," I whisper. "Do you want to get us blown away?"

His face turns into a kid who's just been scolded.

"You're an ace, Castress," I whisper, "But you're gonna get us killed."

Castress makes me wonder, how can I both hate and love a guy at the same time? "Sit tight and don't shoot."

I wiggle the steel pot on his head. Castress is only seventeen and has pimples. He enlisted and volunteered for the infantry and I'm worried because he's over-the-top gung-ho, which is what gets somebody killed. I just hope he won't take anyone with him. Some spit gets caught in my throat worrying about him, and I nod my head into the leaves to let out a cough. I lift my head and look for Rodriguez and spot him flat on the ground in the leaves. He's the farthest on the right flank. I wriggle close enough to whisper, "Don't shoot." He nods and gives me a thumbs up and I head back to Spellbinder to see if he's made contact.

I pass O'Sullivan hunched behind Armaruder who I don't want to talk to. Armaruder never listens anyway. He runs himself like a machine that obeys some ingrained fucked up warrior mentality. But he's been here eighteen months and he's good under pressure. I crawl up next to him to see if he has anything to tell me. He doesn't. He just sits with his eyes glued to an imaginary place beyond the foliage where he is absolutely certain Charlie is. I'd feel better if he wasn't so eager to kill. Still, I don't say anything. I figure Armaruder is okay on his own. He's always okay. He has eighteen confirmed kills and has been wounded three times. I doubt if he'll die in Vietnam. I can't see it happening. God damn him! I shake my head and move on.

Something about Armaruder makes me want to kill the sonofabitch myself.

I tap Catchahorse on the foot as I go by and see him nod.

As I'm shimmying along on my stomach, I have this moment of extreme clarity. These moments seem to come at the oddest times. It's as if I'm holding as many thoughts as I want to, all at once—all perfectly clear—things right in front of me, things half a world away. And in this timeless moment, in this shining clarity with possibly a company or even a regiment of North Vietnamese regulars twenty meters away, crazily, I see Sara, Priscilla's roommate. I think, wouldn't she be proud if she knew I was thinking of her now. She's standing at the front door of the dorm where I'd gone to fuck Priscilla. I hadn't thought to check first and it turned out Priscilla's skiing for the weekend with some guy from Yale.

I ask Sara if I could come up to her room for a smoke. I'd brought along a dime bag of pot. At first she hesitates, but after some convincing I see a spark in her eye and she goes, "Oh, what the hell," and walks me up the stairs. She knows what a big deal it is for the two of us to be alone in their room without Priscilla. And this is the first time I've been there. But it also gives me some real insight into Priscilla to see her part of the room. At the head of her bed leans a bunch of her childhood dolls all in a row against a line of colored pillows. Not just one or two, but nine or ten. Sara says more dolls are under the bed. She says Priscilla switches them in and out, depending if she thinks a doll has been bad.

Remembering that word "bad," brings me back to Armaruder. He's a badass motherfucker and you don't ever want to get in his way.

Sara sits down on the floor and supports her back against the side of her bed. I sit next to her and fumble for about ten minutes trying to roll a joint. I finally give up, embarrassed, and let her do it. The pot is mostly stems and seeds but it brings on a mild high regardless, if not nearly what I'd hoped for. I'm sure my nervousness has something to do with preventing me from feeling high.

Somewhere in our conversation she begins to warm up and lets me put my arm around her shoulders. I feel how loose her body is, which tells me the pot is performing its magic. She lets her head fall back against my arm which I take as a signal that she might be opening up to the idea of us doing something. When I look over at her she is staring aimlessly at the ceiling. She begins to talk about art, which is her major, and tells me how much she admires Picasso for his lack of inhibition more than anything. It surprises me when she says, "You can feel the sexuality in his women," and then turns toward me and I look into her big brown eyes. When I lean over to kiss her she meets me more than halfway.

Sara is much hotter than I could've imagined. She kisses passionately and doesn't wait long before reaching down between my legs and grabbing me. She gets up on her knees, undoes my belt and my zipper, and gives me a professional quality blowjob.

After that we drive into town, buy some beer and return to her room, which now seems to be her room, and fuck three times—once on the rug and twice in her bed.

In the morning both of us feel bad and good about what we've done. Sara has a steady boyfriend, so it isn't like I'm going to break up with Priscilla and start up with her. After a lot of talk and a lot of cigarettes, we decide I won't tell

Priscilla and Sara won't tell her boyfriend. What we've done is a one-time thing that will remain secret.

I think, wouldn't it be great if Sara were here to fuck me now? Wow! Listen to me—wanting to fuck Sara again! But why wouldn't I? She was one of the best fucks I ever had. I wonder if I'll ever see her again. Let a few years pass and you realize who are the ones you really love.

At least that's the way I see it, lying on my belly in the jungle, feeling I might be about to die.

I think of Castress and worry. I imagine his pimply face and pound my forehead with my fist.

Finally, I return to Spellbinder who's curled up around his radio between Zabriski and Jaspon. He wants me to confirm the coordinates for the enemy's position as he reads them off the map. He presses his mouth against the handset and speaks in the perfect quiet voice he's mastered that nobody who's more than a foot away can hear. I lean my head up against his and listen. But for a second he covers the handset and tells me, "They want to know, how many KIA's."

Speaking into the handset, Spellbinder says, "Roger," which is merely a confirmation not an amount. He's playing dumb because he doesn't know what to say. But he isn't stupid because he knows if he tells them "none" they might not take us seriously.

"What's the count?" the radio guy says again.

Finally Spellbinder says, "Beaucoup. Over."

Evidently "beaucoup" settled the matter for the guy because he says, "That's a Roger," then, "Out."

Spellbinder drops his hand with the handset into his lap and looks into my eyes. "They say they're sending a gunship."

We wait.

I sit with Spellbinder and Zabriski on the far side, facing the hill in front. I pull my knees up resting my chin on my hands and stare absently into the holes in the plastic stock of my weapon. The bridge of my nose rests against the metal site on the barrel. As a superstitious ritual brought on by nervousness, I check the bandolier wrapped around my chest, touching each magazine as though each one was a rosary bead, one more precious than the next.

We haven't given away our position.

Maybe Charlie doesn't even know we're here.

Maybe the noise he thought he heard was just an animal.

Nobody shoots.

All is quiet. All is still.

Until we hear the sounds of movement in the thick bush. I'm praying nobody loses his nerve and starts firing. We're dead meat if someone does. It sounds like there are a lot of them and only nine of us.

I leave Spellbinder and crawl as silently as I can over to Armaruder. He's tracking some voices with the muzzle of his carbine stuck into the bushes.

Armaruder is the only one of us who carries a carbine. He says he likes the small size. Watching him with it, he looks like a kid with a toy gun. Only he's real good with it. I've seen him using it. At the moment he's pressing the stock tight against his cheek so the skin is all bunched up and red. He dances the carbine from side to side as if he sees through the wall of leaves in front of him while his eyes jump back and forth like quick cuts between scenes in a movie.

Charlie is getting closer. It is odd and frightening to hear Vietnamese being spoken as clearly now as if we were in the same room. Armaruder looks at me like I'm the enemy. "Listen," he says in his professional whisper.

I ask, "How many do you think?"

He shrugs.

I tell him, "We called in air support."

He shrugs again. What he's telling me without words is: "Who the fuck knows when a chopper will get here? Maybe never."

Armaruder is right, of course. Sometimes we wait for hours before air support shows up. Sometimes we wait and they never come. As in, never.

Suddenly I am shivering because my fatigues are soaked through from sweat and from the stream below the cliff. I shiver wildly for a few minutes before I'm able to stop.

I realize Spellbinder has followed me and crouches at my side like a faithful dog. He knows I'm looking at him and he keeps his face turned away like he's embarrassed. He lifts his nose at a voice we both hear clearly, and points at the invisible hillside beyond the bushes.

I aim my weapon inches off Armaruder's shoulder. It sounds like a stream of NVA advancing down the hill. I feel Armaruder's breath in my ear. "They're coming straight down on top of us," he says as if he can actually see them. I almost believe he can.

"Don't shoot," I whisper, frantic with cusped words. "There's no way out of here."

He looks back at me the way a kindergarten teacher looks at a kid who's just peed in his pants and shakes his head. "Maybe they'll just go away."

In his eyes is the wrath of a man hungry for human blood. I do my best to give him a look I think could kill such a man. I know I need to get away from Armaruder before I explode. Carrying my anger with me, I low-crawl away while I drag my rifle behind, catching mouthfuls of wet leaves and dirt. When I'm far enough away for Armaruder not to hear, I stop. Spellbinder stops.

I realize I've lost it.

Suddenly, there is a volley of shots from the NVA somewhere high up.

"Who the hell did you have on the radio?" I burrow into Spellbinder's eyes.

"They're dispatching a gunship. Call sign Red Tail."

Before I can say anything, an explosion rips the damp air into pieces. A flash of heat from an Apache's rocket tears the leaves off the bushes between the trail and us and plasters them on our skin. I picture the leaves that pass by, us fluttering over the edge of the ridge, falling like rose petals sprinkled on somebody's beautiful bride.

(kids in kindergarten sing this while tossing petals in the air)

Then I hear Armaruder firing.

I know it makes him happy. Another chance to chalk up kills.

The next sounds I hear through the ringing in my ears are Zabriski and Jaspon pulling even bursts of twos and threes. I grope in the leaves for my weapon, push the crud from the barrel, turn it full-auto and aim at the sounds of Charlie's AK-47's. I drop my first mag, rip another from the bandolier and jam it in. As I start toward Jaspon, a round lifts the leaves beside me. Zabriski crawls up, circles around, and disappears through the bushes to our right. He's gone for a while and just when I think of going after him he comes crawling backwards through the bushes like a lizard who's lost his tail. "Fucking Christ," he moans in the way someone does who's just seen something he can't comprehend. "It's right, fucking, there. No more than five meters from here." He shakes his head. It's like somebody's handed him a million dollar bill, and he can't really believe it.

He has something more to say. "Sarge, Rodriguez and Castress went out on the trail...."

"What the fuck? Why?"

"Castress crawled out there. Rodriguez went after him."

"Shit. Are they dead?"

He remains frozen. He wants to say more but can't.

"They gotta be."

Again, my mind goes perfectly clear. I know we've got to get them before the gunship makes another pass. The Apache's more dangerous than Charlie. I turn to Spellbinder. "Contact Red Tail. Repeat the coordinates. Make sure he gets it."

Spellbinder fumbles with the radio dial searching for the gunship's frequency.

"I'm gonna have a look," I tell Zabriski. "Keep firing. But keep it high."

I'm thankful to hear Armaruder's fast bursts coming from the far right. I start moving forward grabbing Spellbinder's shirt, pulling him after me to keep the radio close. I want to talk to the chopper pilot if he shows up when I'm out on the trail. Digging an elbow into the dirt, I lunge us forward. Suddenly there's light coming through the leaves. I push forward and see the trail.

It's a simple two-track road with a grass center. Two bodies lie face down on the grass, flat and disheveled. Their clothes are shredded. Because of the way they look, I can't help it but my mind turns the bodies into two American flags, all shot up. Stars and Stripes Forever. Tiny pieces showering the Fourth of July parade like confetti.

Sometimes, I hate what the mind does.

Charlie is taking potshots at the bodies. They're the only visible targets. It's awful, even for a few seconds, to watch the bullets make the bodies jump.

I have to control myself from yelling, STOP!!

My mind is blank. I am paralyzed. We sit simply breathing, counting second upon second. Cold beads of sweat drip beneath my wet fatigues, making me shudder.

Then we hear the gunship in the distance. It's coming back. Fuck! It will rip the bodies apart! The sound of the blades chopping the air echoes between the mountains. We hear it turn and head back toward us.

The Apache overflies the trail making an observation run. No mini-gun, just a blast of noise and a down-blast from the blades. But it's enough to keep Charlie quiet.

Armaruder suddenly appears on the trail, grabs both bodies by their shirts and drags them back.

My heart beats like a drum as he runs. Then halts as he makes it back into the brush. Then resumes a steady beat.

I've just witnessed something beautiful.

The Apache appears overhead again. This time it hovers above the trail looking like some sort of evil science fiction death machine and spits a solid red line from its nose into the hill on the other side. It's not shooting at the trail, its mini-gun moves back and forth tearing up the trees like a mad giant with lightning-fast pruning shears. Charlie can't escape the Apache. After what he's done to my two men, in my mind's eye I gloat, picturing thousands of bullets tearing him apart.

Spellbinder and I move back into the cover. I leave him again, and find Armaruder. He's poised like a cat staring down the barrel of his carbine. O'Sullivan is beside him and a little behind as if paying deference.

The two dead bodies are a clump in the leaves behind

them.

I want to say something to Armaruder but can't. He feels my gaze and keeps his eyes turned away.

We stop shooting, except Armaruder, at clock-like intervals, flings a round into the jungle. Since it's Armaruder, I imagine the bullets flying straight into some dead NVA's gaping mouth. I fully believe he can do it.

The radio squawks. Major Fuckworth wants us to retreat.

"Bring your people back," he says in his best radio voice like he's singing a freedom song like, *We Shall Overcome,* or *Make Freedom Ring,* or *Go Tell It on the Mountain.*

"Pull back down the ridge, we're gonna soften up the trail. We're calling in F-4's."

It's like Duckworth's voice is being transmitted from another planet.

Doesn't he fucking KNOW?

That two of us are dead.

That Charlie is hamburger meat.

Doesn't he know what the bombs will do?

I hear him yell, "Pull back now, Goddamn it!"

"Yes, Sir!"

I got your point, Major.

I drop the handset into Spellbinder's palm, wishing I could let go of the war just as easily.

This bullshit war that's run from far away.

From where the majors and colonels in base camp never get to see your buddies riddled with bullets, from someplace where they get to wipe their asses with toilet paper on a roll every day.

When I check my watch it's exactly 0800 hours. Breakfast time back home. The kids have finished their orange juice and Rice Krispies and everyone's heading out of the house. Dad's off to work. Mom kisses him goodbye and the kids head out to the sidewalk carrying their lunchboxes to wait for the school bus.

(the kids are singing something back home, but I can't hear what it is)

All together, we drag the riddled bodies back behind Jaspon's position to the edge of the cliff and start down. Under sparkling bars of sunlight we lower ourselves from the edge of the ridge feeling for footholds.

The bombs hit before we even hear the Phantom jets. The ground comes alive like it's dancing the conga. The rock wall shakes so it's all we can do to hold on. After the first bombs hit we can hardly hear. The blasts leave only a high-pitched ring in the ears.

We have a strong need to get down the cliff but the bodies slow us down. Each of them is wrapped in a poncho held between two men. O'Sullivan and Zabriski have one; Armaruder and I have the other. It's difficult to remember which body is which because they both feel more like pulp. Partway down, the body Armaruder and I carry slips out of the poncho. It's gone before Armaruder or I can do anything about it and it wedges itself behind a small tree and hangs from its armpits. We can see it's Rodriguez's body just as the Phantom jets drop two more bombs on the trail that makes the body do a shimmy, nodding its head up and down. It drops a little and is caught again by its arms now flung upward as in some crazy gesture: Praise the Lord!

All this, for what?

The super secret listening device must be smashed to smithereens by our own Phantom Jets.

Neither of us wants to deal with Rodriguez's body. Part of me says, he's dead so what does it matter?

But why do my eyes heat up?
Why are they wet?

Catchahorse helps us extricate Rodriguez's body from the branch and wrap it back in the poncho, all the time while clinging precariously to the rock. Armaruder ties a piece of green parachute cord around the neck. As I stuff an arm in the poncho I brush what I think is a leech off the back of my neck. But touching it, I realize it's a piece of Rodriguez's skin.

I push it off and let out a dry wretch.

Catchahorse helps Armaruder and me get a firm hold. I watch Armaruder strain and show his big white teeth like he's on a toothpaste commercial on Tee Vee. Seeing him up close, I know he's not smiling; his mouth is frozen in place from the effort and the concussion from the bombs.

We inch down the slippery rock now with the poncho pressed between our bodies. Soggy clumps of moss slide away from the rocks beneath our feet. We find cracks and small trees to hold onto. About ten meters from the bottom my bicep cramps and the weight of the body begins to pull us both off the cliff. Armaruder is pulled toward me and loses his hold. I catch him by the shoulder but can't hold his weight and the body. Armaruder knows it too, and to save ourselves we both make the decision without speaking to let the body drop. The poncho opens up like a cape and drops with the body. The body lands sideways. Its skull cracks on a boulder in the stream below.

The others have made it down with Castress's body. They watch Rodriguez's body fall onto the rocks in the stream, the dead crack echoing like a shot into everyone's head. When Armaruder and I are down, I see the others standing motionless, staring down at their feet.

We wrap up the bodies again and start downhill in the

streambed. Moving is slow because the stones are slippery but nobody minds.

Two hours later we stop in a clearing of elephant grass and Spellbinder calls for a dustoff chopper to pick up the bodies and take us to Chu Lai. When it shows up an hour later my eyes fix on the red cross in the white square on its nose, which looks to me at that moment like the most beautiful piece of artwork on Earth. Like it should be hanging in the Louvre in Paris. I flash on an image of the statue of the Winged Victory!

We lift the ponchos for the last time and a couple of medics pull them onto the chopper floor. They help lift Zabriski, who can't move one arm. Then Catchahorse, O'Sullivan and Jaspon climb aboard. The chopper is maxed out with weight so the pilot lifts off.

Three of us are left behind. Spellbinder, Armaruder and me are tucked safely inside the thick grass where we wait for the next dustoff.

Armaruder has some cigarettes and he and I smoke, letting the smoke and the hot sun heal us.

On the radio they tell us they have only one chopper available—the one that just came and went—and that we'll have to sit tight until it returns. So we sit there for a couple of hours without talking. I lie back against my pack and think about my bedroom at home. I think about the only girl I ever fucked in my bed. When that no longer works I think about pictures of works of art that I used to cut from books and magazines and hang on the wall.

When the chopper shows up, the medics pull us aboard. The metal floor is covered with blood. I don't want to touch it but my fatigues are already soaked with blood so it doesn't fucking matter.

From the open door I watch the jungle pass under us until I switch for a second to watch Armaruder's face. The look in his eyes is motionless, even as the skin on his face vibrates from the chopper. Looking out again, I see we're flying south across the wide sweep of the sea with lines of waves coming in towards shore. The waves hypnotize me. It seems as if they hold some important cosmic message but I have no idea what it is.

I think how nice it would feel to slip off the cold floor and dive into the sea. Sinking under the water, I imagine my rifle becoming heavier and heavier as it weighs me down. I know I can let go but I don't. Instead I float down toward the bottom with a beautiful transparent grace. I reach the bottom where the fish, dressed in bright fluorescent colors, greet me with their swirly tails just above the white sandy ocean floor.

I steal another quick look at Armaruder and wonder how I could've been so wrong about somebody.

The first sergeant hands me my wallet.
Of course I check the contents.

A card inside:

M16 Rifle Cleaning Tips

The M16 is the finest military rifle ever made. It's lightweight, easy to handle, and will put out a lot of lead. If you know it, respect it, and treat it right, it will be ready when you need it. The following tips are from combat veterans who wanted to pass on to you their ideas on weapon care. Learn 'em, use 'em, and you'll not be caught short!

A. Keep your ammo and magazine as clean and dry as possible. Lightly lube the magazine spring only. Oil it up, and you're headed for trouble.

B. Inspect your ammo when you load the magazines. Don't use dented or dirty ammo. Remember, load only 18 or 19 rounds.

C. Clean your rifle every chance you get. 3-5 times a day will not be too often in some cases. Cleanliness is next to godliness, boy, and it may save your life!

D. Be sure to clean carbon and dirt from those barrel locking lugs. Pipe cleaners help here and in the gas port.

E. Don't be bashful about asking for cleaning materials when you need 'em. They're available: get 'em and use 'em.

F. Check your extractor and spring often: if they are worn or burred, get new ones ASAP.

G. Lube your rifle using only LSA. That's the best. A light coat put on with a rag after cleaning is good. Functional parts need generous applications often.

Put a very light coat of LSA in the bore and chamber after cleaning.

Sun's in
Sun's out.

It's hot again. Not long ago our landing zone was all soup and slime and shit. Now, it's baked solid as a piecrust. Our feet no longer sink in and make sucking sounds when we walk—suuuuck, suuuuck—now they clump, clump, bump, bump against the hard dirt floor. And we get to take our shirts off and dry our boots and dry out the rot between our toes and drrrrryyyyy the fuck out. The hot sun feels good and comes up and goes down and turns into night and we fit into a grunt's routine of cleaning our weapons and washing our socks and underwear and jungle fatigues and loading and reloading our magazines and smoking until we pass out and saddling up in the morning and heading out on patrol.

Even in the friendly villes where the young men are called Popular Forces, they're on our side during the day and turn into VC when the sun goes down. Charlie owns all the territory. He owns us, too. Because of some bullshit agreement between our governments we are obligated to get permission from the local village chiefs before using their land. Which means the village chief gets paid a tidy sum to let us patrol in his village. So the VC know what we're doing even before we do it. What a way to run a war. Real slick, General   Go-Fuck-Yourself-And-The-Horse-You-Rode-In-On! So, do we wonder why the VC lie in wait and attempt to ambush us as we enter their villes? Usually it's just the local snipers, some young kids who can hardly hold a weapon, who try to scare us away. Of course, we're expecting them, and since we are hip to them being tipped off, we've learned to ask for permission for places we never intend to go. We go where we want to "by mistake." Ha! Charlie's not the only tricky one.

The French left a lot of children behind. Some of the most beautiful Vietnamese girls look like they could've grown up in Paris. The French fought a long time here and what did it get them? Nothing except all these beautiful children left behind. I'm always thinking about stuff like that—about everything, really. I know that too much thinking puts you out of touch. When you start thinking what this is all about, you always come to the same conclusion: it's all for shit and none of it—none of it, not one stitch—is worth seeing your friends die or seeing your legs blown off—for what? So some fucking politician can keep the war machine going in his state. I think of South Carolina where I trained, where practically the whole state is owned by the military. Fort Jackson takes up half the state and Charleston is a huge Navy base. Probably the only ones who don't profit from the war are us lowly grunts who do everyone's dirty work for shit an hour—and, of course, for the incredible glory of it all. Fucking-A! We might win a medal. What a crock of shit. The people back home—the ones we are supposedly fighting for—don't want us here. The people who live here don't want us here. So who are we fighting for? What are we fighting for? All I can figure is we're fighting for our own lives, our friends' lives, just to make it through our tour—our "365 and a wake up"—and to come home alive.

First lieutenant shoots dog
(man's best friend)

I wake up this morning with that nervous twitch that every grunt gets sometime during his time in-country. Watching my fingers tremble holding a cigarette, I know I've got it so bad that it's time to check myself out of the field before I'm jinxed and checked out permanently.

I find the lieutenant on the way to the crapper and tell him I'm moving off the LZ. I tell him I'm getting very paranoid and I know of a place to stay where I'll be a helluva lot safer than on fucking LZ Zebra. I'm naïve enough to think he's going to be sympathetic because he knows I'm a short-timer.

This is (sort of) how our conversation goes:

"Sir," I begin smiling, feeling he will be reasonable. "You know, I've been out here too long and I've got the shakes pretty bad…"

He interrupts. I can tell by his eyes, he doesn't want to hear anything I have to say.

"Jones," he begins in a voice that is all business. "At about 0600 this morning I received word that the 1st of the 53rd ran into an NVA basecamp out by the border. I received orders to supply one or two experienced troops that can tell them what they ran into and lead them to the ones who left in such a hurry. The dumb shits in the 1st of the 53rd don't know their asses from holes in the ground."

Obviously I know what is coming next and I start to rattle in my jungle boots right in front of him like I'm a depth charge about to explode.

"So I want you and Catchahorse to check out the basecamp and tell the dumb fucks what they found and show them where Charlie's hiding before they get their asses whipped."

By this point I'm convinced he's crazy. And he's not done; he's just getting warmed up. "They're stuck out there under triple canopy and they can't cut a landing zone. So we're gonna have you rappel in from a chopper. 1st of the 53rd will cover you from the ground. (Remember, the lieutenant just said they don't know their asses from a hole in the ground.) "Have you ever rappelled before?" he asks perfectly seriously, as if I'm John Wayne's sidekick and might want to do my own stunts.

"Sir," I'm visibly quaking now, "What I was telling you before is that I've got the shakes so bad that if you honestly think I'm going to dangle from some rope while Charlie does target practice on my ass, well..." My anger is bubbling to the surface now. "Sir..." I try to make it sound as polite as possible. "Fuck you," Then I add, "sir," just to show him I'm army all the way through.

His eyes go red and he almost spits. "Why you, shit you. What do you think you're doing, sergeant?"

"Disobeying an order, Sir."

"I'm going to hand you your ass—with a court martial shoved up it."

"Be my guest, sir. Look..." I say, trying to reason with him when I should know better. "I'm two months short. I've got the shakes. I'll take the court martial. Have it gift wrapped, sir."

If I end up in the brig at least I'll be alive.

"Why you...Goddamn fucking..."

I turn around and tell him over my shoulder, "I'll be somewhere in South Vietnam if you want me."

"Look, sergeant. Do you know how deep a pile of shit you're walking into?"

"Yessir, you're standing in it yourself. I can smell it."

As I walk away, my anger turns to all-smiles. God, I'm feeling better already. He's screaming his fool head off somewhere behind me and I know I've won, and he does too.

"I'll be wiping my ass with your stripes."

"Yessir, whatever you like. Have a good crap."

"Go fuck yourself, sergeant—you haven't heard the last of me."

"Sir, you can tell the whole world about me," I yell back with a smile on my face. "They'd probably like hearing my story."

As I turn to look back again, I see him in the crouched position, which is as much of a natural reflex to us all now as taking a pee. But instead of aiming his .45 pistol at me, I see he's taking a bead on a dog that belongs to Cookie.

Just as I'm thinking he's only pretending, he pulls the trigger and hits the dog between the eyes. Pink brain bits make a tiny cloud where the dog's head was. The pup holds it together on all fours for a few seconds still standing and looking like he's about to chase after a cat or something. Then his legs go weak and he falls over on his side.

I feel my hand reach down for my .45. It's that automatic response that happens to the good guy in B-westerns. But instead I turn on my heel like I'm on parade and keep on walking untill I'm out of camera range.

I move in with Delph Connor on the base back in Chu Lai. Not into his hootch, where all these dangerous desktop warriors have shiny new guns they've never fired unless they've killed somebody by mistake, but into his office next to the commanding general's. I set up a cot—the one Connor uses for screwing the CO's hootch girl behind his detail desk—and build a kind of bunker out of filing cabinets and cardboard boxes stuffed with papers. As paranoid as I am, I sleep with Maybelline, my M16 beside me, with a round in the chamber and my .45 under my pillow with my hand touching it.

During the day I walk on the beach and eat hamburgers and drink beer at the bamboo USO stand. And feel the breeze off the China Sea and listen to it rustling the straw roof.

Days file in;
days file out.

There's the smell of freedom in the air by the sea. The sound of the rolling waves keeps me in a permanent state of mindlessness. I spend hours walking on the beach. Now that I'm getting to know it, I realize it's about the best beach I've ever seen anywhere. It's a crescent with palm trees and powdery white sand. Up close the water is clear and turns to turquoise blue out toward the horizon. It's always the perfect temperature for swimming if you don't mind the sharks.

I try to knock coconuts out of the trees by throwing rocks thinking, if I only could use my M16! Once when I was drunk I tried to climb up the trunk of a palm and fell off. The only coconut I ever got I bought from a Vietnamese girl selling them from a basket on the beach.

I find the Alexandria Quartet by Lawrence Durrell in the USO library. I started to read it back in South Carolina but didn't get very far. Now, I lie on my olive drab towel imagining myself in Egypt with Balthazar and the others having sex with Justine. I smolder away my days drinking Absinthe and smoking opium, having conversations about Moorish architecture. Durrell himself shows up, and Cavafy is there and some other great poets—maybe even some beats like Gregory Corso, Lawrence Ferlinghetti, and Alan Ginsburg who's howling away. Of course Henry Miller is there, having just sailed over from Marseille or somewhere. Gertrude Stein hosts parties with Picasso, and his nude models are all over the place.

When the sun is too hot on the sand I dive into the crystal-clear sea and play with the jellyfish. There are infinite numbers of them. They're not the stinging kind, so GI's throw them at each other like snowballs. Someone has a big two or three pound one and tries to start a game of football.

I swim away. I dive under water and watch the jellyfish for as long as I can hold my breath until I start to feel like a jellyfish myself. I find I can actually hang in the water the way they do, suspended halfway between sinking and floating while letting the sea push me toward the beach.

At one point some guys come running over. I hear them yelling even from under the water but I don't realize that they're yelling at me. They think I've drowned. They dive in and swim up to me and start to pull me in toward shore. Two guys grab me by each arm—and I feel for a few moments the way a drowning man would. They handle me real rough because when you're dead, you're an inanimate object like a tire and they figure nothing is going to hurt you even if you get dragged over some rocks.

Now, I think, I know what it feels like to be dead.

Rodriguez and Castress flash through my head.

"Let me go!" I yell. "I'm alive!"

Despite my protests they drag me onto the beach and are all pissed off when I sit up and tell them, "I was pretending I was a jellyfish."

It's no joke to be pretending to play dead in Vietnam.

"Shit," one says.

"Shit," another one says.

I feel bad for a second. Then dive back in to join the jellyfish.

Beside the runway
United States Air Force Base, Chu Lai —

There's no fence to keep me away so I'm standing so close I have to cover my ears as the roar of the F4 Phantoms blast the top off my head. The planes are very beautiful. They're like arrowheads with wings, their noses sharp as a razor for slicing through the air. I love looking at them—I could stand here all day. They taxi down the runway towards me on tiny little wheels, delicate as ballerina's shoes, belying the powerful bodies they carry along with these huge rockets under their wings. They always fly in pairs when they do airstrikes. Now, with their canopies open, I can see the two crewmen inside. I wave. They wave. The pilot gives a thumbs up and they pull the canopy down, or it comes down hydraulically (I don't know which). I cover my ears when they begin to move down the runway—starting with a slow crawl that becomes a rush until suddenly they're speeding like a bat out of hell. The afterburners kick in and two red-orange flames shoot from the back like giant blowtorches, then the nose jerks up real quick and they take off almost straight up into the sky. In an instant they flip onto their sides—first one, then the other—heading west and disappear into the clouds over the mountains.

Seeing the Phantoms makes me miss my friends, my squad. I think maybe it's too soon for me to leave them. I never told them goodbye so I could just show up again and they'd hardly know I've been gone. It's been less than a week.

Heading across the runway I think maybe I've just been getting some R&R—some days away from the madness. Suddenly I'm standing in front of a huge open hanger with a C130 parked inside. Then I see what it is. It's a plane full of dead bodies. I wretch and suck my stomach in to keep from puking but the taste of puke's already in my mouth. I ask myself, why am I standing here on this steaming hot runway, looking into the open-ended asshole of this huge aircraft with all these neat rows of black plastic body bags lined up on aluminum racks like trays in the mess hall? Why do I have to be here at this moment to see this awful sight when I can't possibly understand what it all means and who the fuck they are inside, and who the fuck they were?

Some guys from Miami or Duluth or Cincinnati or St. Louis or I don't know where.

I want to tiptoe beyond this point, "all present and accounted for," as the drill sergeant tells the lieutenant when he's got his training company all lined up. I want to get away quickly to where there's no need to look anymore into the asshole of this great silver flying machine with its giant floppy wings that is being loaded by some young privates and corporals who have pulled the shittiest duty on the planet.

But I feel I must stand at attention before I leave—to give a final salute to the bodies inside that were once fighting men.

Don't ask me why, but suddenly I think of freezing my ass off at Fort Dix, New Jersey at 0530 hours, standing in formation before the sun is up while the dumb Fifth-Grade educated nincompoop drill sergeant decides whether we will have our ear-flaps up on our caps or down on our caps. (I have no idea why he thinks they all must be the same.)

While we wait for the sergeant to gather the two thoughts together and make a fucking choice, we are getting frostbitten ears.

But here I am, now a sergeant, sweating from the heat, standing at attention at an airbase in Vietnam, staring into the gaping mad hole of this dark crazed death plane getting frostbitten eyes!

When there's a war on, living is no fun.
When there's a war on, you can't see the sun.

The hate of the people of America has spread here through their open pores. They could not bear the sight of a war going on in Nantucket...

...in Los Angeles
...in Racine
...in Miami
...So, they fly their hate over here.

Song My, Vietnam: It is nothing like America. Except of course, there are people who wash their clothes—
and sit down to dinner each night
and sleep
and dream
and pray
and go to church
and are afraid of dying.

I must go back to my friends.

Taken hostage
In this Godforsaken land.

Yes, I succumbed—I went back out to Indian Country to the 1st of the 53rd who were still hunkered down near a NVA base camp.

I admit, I was to chickenshit not too.

The crazy lieutenant threatened me with the one thing he knew would work. He was gonna keep me hostage in Vietnam. The lieutenant sent the first sergeant to find me. He told me the lieutenant was dead set on making certain that I'd never get my orders to DEROS if I didn't take Catchahorse and fly out to help the fuckers.

DEROS means: "Date Estimated Return (from) Overseas." They cut an official set of orders for those still alive after eleven months and hand 'em to you when you're two weeks short so you can make the rounds of all the places you need to get signed off from: like from the brigade surgeon, who needs to make sure you don't take some communicable disease back home. Everybody knows someone who got held in-country because of syphilis. They keep you here for three months to make sure you're not going to infect some pretty college girls up at Vassar. Not that a Vassar or Sarah Lawrence or even a state college girl is going to consider giving a veteran the time of day. We've all heard the stories about soldiers returning stateside who get spit on and called "baby killers" and shit like that. Thank you very much, America, for your deep appreciation of the job we do. Love ya for that!

So if I ever want to see the promised land, I have to obey the lieutenant's orders.

He has me by the balls.

Fucker.

Should've shot the cocksucker after he shot Cookie's

dog. Nobody would've blamed me. Not one single soul.

So I dangle down from a Huey over the jungle to help out a bunch of sorry ass grunts (who don't know their asses from a VC hole in the ground). We find a huge basecamp in an underground tunnel complex (for the last week everything above ground has been bombed to shit). I have some guys move a rice pot and, sure e-nough, there is a tunnel entrance. We send down a tunnel rat, who looks to be about four-foot three and, sure enough, he finds that tunnel leads to another and another. He finds a whole arsenal down there.

This is a list of what we find:
29 Chicom hand grenades
thousands of small arms rounds
39 new SKS rifles
8 carbines
2 M-1 rifles
32 WP rounds
11 Swiss submachine guns
1 U.S. burp gun
30 RPG's
30 U.S. Claymores
64 Chinese 82mm mortar shells
15,000 Chinese machine gun rounds
1 M16
no packs, no rice, no clothes,
no Charlie

**The days are long
But it is the night that has to be coped with.**

I sail across the American landscape.

The days are long but it is mostly the night that has to be coped with.

The guards are settling down. They beat sandbags into comfortable shapes to lie on. Everybody cleans his weapon. Everybody reads Spiderman...and hopes for the moon to be large.

Transistors whisper.

A wild boar moves through the brush.

Everybody watches and listens. Nobody shoots.

I think of it like this: you can see the killing but never death. Not until you die.

I comb my hair.

I write a letter.

It is always done in this order.

I must remember not to get excited about anything while in Vietnam.

I get three letters from the states. In each one is a package of Kool-Aid. Two grape, one lime.

It's my birthday, so I light a pack of matches…
Then blow them out.

This is a moment when loneliness is like an empty glass.

Just to see how I'd feel, I write a letter to a girl who doesn't know I'm in Vietnam. I ask her out for Friday night. Say I'll be in town. I spend the rest of the night drinking and wondering whether or not to mail it.

The Village awakens. Papa-san is a mechanical rhythm. Children and babies. Children and babies. A girl presses out the folds on her blouse. Mama-san has purple teeth. Village filled with grime. Shit and dust. Girl with long, long fingernails. She carries sandbags for two cents a bag. Her little brother, Baby-san, says, "Wanna boom-boom my seesta? My seesta real nice, GI."

Picture in today's Stars and Stripes: Tuesday Weld barbequing hamburgers in her backyard in a bikini.
Watch out for the hot grease, Tuesday.
Don't want to burn your tummy.

Bombs fall, and I try to get high.
Bombs fall, and I try to get high.
Bombs fall, and Charlie tries to get high.

You don't see any expensive cars around here.
So no worry about getting the paint scratched.
No Cadillacs.

No Lincolns.

Not many Rolls Royces or Bentleys.

Reginald, would you bring my mind around to the front door. I'd like to ride into town.

The girl does not know I know how large her tits are.

I see her in Queen Teen Magazine.

She is naked from the knees up.

A mortar lands where I stood six minutes ago.

I look over my shoulder to ponder my dead self.

We had no signs of an attack.

Someone who I didn't know lost half his head.

One guy is carried to the medic with his skin falling off. He doesn't feel anything. He has no eyes. He has eyes but they do not see. The medic cuts off his skin with a pair of scissors. The guy is pink underneath.

An armored personnel carrier backs up quickly, running over a grunt. We're called grunts because of the noise we make. I've heard the sound. It's an apt name although I like to think I'm more than just the sound I make. Could just as easily be a burp, a fart, a cough. A laugh might be nice. People could say, "Here comes a group of laughs." Or, "That guy over there— he's a real laugh." Hahahahahahaha. Only the guy isn't laughing.

His body is cut in half.

We don't even get to shoot back. It was just the usual. A nighttime mortar attack.

Once again, we sit and watch the gunships piss red rounds.

(seems like we do this a lot)

The kitchen tent is shattered.

I think back (fondly) to my days in the hospital with malaria.

I beg the mosquitos to bite me.
We walk…as gently as tea is poured into a cup.

On patrol
Near Hill 361

We find a girl shot in the pussy. She is still alive but her pussy is sticking right out of her pants and some of it is splattered on the sand. There is very little blood, hardly any at all, like she is only bleeding internally. Her hands are so fine, and not at all like a working girl's hands or a girl who is in a war.

"She carried a weapon," they keep telling me, but I just look off through the trees and stare.

Since I'm the sergeant, I'm the one they go to—like I'm supposed to know something they do not. MOTHER-FUCKER!!!

I'm getting angrier and angrier, as you can see. I've got so few days left that each one is filled with infinite moments which means an infinite amount of shit I have to feel.

Sometimes it scares me the realness with which I was born.
Sometimes it scares me the realness of how easy it is to die.

We have a new roof on our school.
We have a new roof on our school.
We have a new roof on our school.
Three times the VC blew it away.
Blew it away.
Blew it away.
Blew it away.
We have a new roof on our school.
(Vietnamese kids sing this on the way to their bombed-out school)

This is the first time, ever, I've seen the bright yellow halo that rides above a person's head. I see it first on Jaspon. Above his big brown head. I almost don't believe it until I see it again on Catchahorse.

I find your world once again possible to write to.
I now understand the precious practical urgency of remaining on earth.

I will dictate my words
And they will be written in heaven.

A reporter for Time Magazine
Asks me what I think.

A reporter is here. From Time magazine.
I smile and light a cigarette.
Offer him one.
But what do you think? He says
I don't quite think.
He scoffs at me. Walks off.
Maybe you can find Che Guevara.
He'd tell you what he thinks.

The Time man is back for chow.
He sits beside me with his cassette turned on.
He thinks I don't notice,
So I pretend I don't.
He tells me he's from St. Paul, Minnesota.
(making light conversation to suck me in)
Isn't that in America?
I lived in America once.
Until it disowned me.
(sent me to this fucked up place and said it never wanted
to see me again)

A leech is crawling on his pant leg. Should I tell him?
He asks,
What is it?
An inch-worm.
What is your job here?
Getting background for my movie.
Oh, I see.
It's a romance.
Interesting. What did you study in school?
I got drafted instead.

You seem so anti-war.
I'm not anti-anything. What's war?
But why don't you tell me what you think?
I tell him, I would if I could think.

**All these hollow legs around here
Could drive a guy crazy.**

It's like you never know where anybody's hiding his stash. I, particularly, hide my mind with my stash...so as not to be found with it on my person. It's a lot safer leaving my mind behind, especially when I'm in the boonies.
At least if I'm gonna get wasted my mind will live on.

Minds are touchy things, as you probably know. Shake one up a little too much and it's bound to explode.

Instinct is a thing apart.

Here's a general rule: In war you cultivate your instinct, ruin your nervous system and leave your mind wherever you choose. Look at it like this: one way or the other you're going to lose your mind. It's safest to put it aside while you still have it, then you know where to pick it up when it's time to leave.

I find it quite comfortable to live without my mind.

(even for extended periods of time)

And you don't need your mind to laugh.

(the heart is what does the laughing and the crying)

War is the biggest damn drama, comedy, tragedy, farce the mind ever invented. It's lucky we have hearts to ease the pain.

**The world is shooting-up something—
Into its arms, its legs.**

The little rice paddy village of huts we built of ponchos and banana leaves secrete the foulest odors of all life on earth (of death), and I roam around between them endeavoring to be...NON ATTACHABLE to any of it.

Somebody shouts something about a bamboo viper in a clump of bamboo in the middle of our night laager. Five or six guys rush over with machetes in their hands.
I rush over with just my hands.

Camped beside a rice paddy
The general's chopper is arriving.

Chucka, chucka, chucka.

Here comes the new commanding general. He wants to see how his war is going.

Like a great, movie set windstorm fan, his chopper settles upon us and everybody runs to grab hold of what is left of the bunkers we've spent the week constructing. But in thirty seconds, the general's chopper levels our camp.

Great tactician, this general.

He doesn't wait for the chopper to touch down. He's got his entrance rehearsed with the pilot who settles within a yard of the ground. Then, swagger stick in hand, he, the redheaded fool (calls himself the Red Baron), executes a flying leap (Airborne Commando style) down to earth. Only, misjudging the amount of water in the ground, he sinks knee deep in the mud so his aide has to politely assist the fucker in unsticking himself.

We, none of us, can hold our laughter back. The general's face turns as red as the top of his head, and we go back to the task of rebuilding our bunkers. He notices the ragged shape our camp is in and wants to know how we can live in such a mess. The first sergeant politely points out the power of the general's prop wash.

The general mutters something like the Lone Ranger might who has just walked into town having forgotten his mask.

While the general is on the ground for his three minute inspection his chopper circles overhead doing "an observation run," which, in reality, means providing cover for the old man's priceless (according to the army) ass.

A grunt is worth 50,000 dollars.

(that's what it costs to train a man to lose his mind)

How much would a general be worth?
A million, I'm sure.
(at least as much as a chopper anyhow)

All day long there has been an innocent-looking Vietnamese farmer toiling in the rice paddy alongside our camp. He seems like he must be a hundred years old. He is beautiful though. During lunch chow I watched him raking his rice paddy with such care. I was taken by how skillfully the beautiful farmer moved, in such perfect accord with his surroundings that it looked as if he wasn't moving at all. Like a bird gliding with the wind that need never move its wings.

While the general is visiting and his chopper is circling, the chopper suddenly swoops down, and we all watch in horror as one of the general's door gunners blows the farmer away. He does it with a burst from an M60 machine gun he's holding in his lap.

The killing of the farmer
Makes everyone sick.
(we all want to kill the door gunner—and maybe the general too!)

You might ask me how men with no minds can die so easily of a broken heart.
(only if you did not remember what I have already told you)

Men with no minds live totally within their hearts.

The mind killed the beautiful farmer.
The heart is not capable of such brutality.
FOR NO EVIL CAN EXIST IN THE HEART!
GOD LIVES IN THE HEART!

GOD IS PERFECT!
GOD IS ALL GOOD!
ALL LOVING!
ALL MERCIFUL!
ALL LOVE!
WE ARE…
(all of us in this platoon)
ALL!
LOVE!

I need to see God's face
To know He's with me now.

Funny that it's war that is turning us on
To God.

It is pretty hard to see it all happening—that's for sure. Nonetheless, it is happening whether we see it or not.

I think it is true: war speeds up evolution.

A siren screams in the cosmos—
The policemen of love run red lights.

(the jump rope girls sing my Special Orders)
  • I will always present a neat military
appearance.
  • I will always conduct myself in
a soldierly manner and
  • I will do all I can to bring credit upon
myself, my unit and the military service.
  • I will guard everything within the limits of my post
and quit my post only when properly relieved.
  • As a member of the US military forces I will comply
with the Geneva Prisoner of War Convention of 1949. I can
and will:
  • Disarm my prisoner
  • Immediately search him thoroughly
  • Require him to be silent ("Dung noi chuyen")
  • Never mistreat my prisoner
  • Never humiliate or degrade him.

(the girls in kindergarten sing this)
(shush…listen, and you can hear them)

I have seen so many movies where the soldiers die but
where you know as soon as the director yells, "Cut!" the
dead guys will jump up and run over to the canteen to grab
a coffee and Danish.

Why doesn't that happen here? Why can't all my
friends—Castress and Rodriguez and Bailey and Trainer
and Haney—get up and run for a coffee and a Danish?
God, I'll go crazy thinking like this.

But my mind wants to travel backwards, to live in the
past (like a movie) where it knows it's safe because all the

events, no matter how sad, have already happened.

The faint breaking of artillery echoes in the valley between the hills, but even from here, I can hear it.

0630 hours. 50 rounds of mixed mortar fire, 60 & 82mm

RPG's. About 40
Followed by a ground attack all the way 'round the hill.
2 sapper companies with AK-47's & 44's
Beer can Chicom grenades
Scrap lumber laid over wire
About 200 ground forces infiltrated
Killed 27
Bodies were all the way 'round the hill
Claymores
Found one hand in wire
One leg
VC attacked, entered 2 bunkers

Bodies all the way 'round the hill.
(girls and boys sing this)

Friendly mortars fire illumination rounds
70 rounds, 4.2
155 arty then takes over
Medevacs and gunships approach from west
Blow bunkers with suspected unfriendlies to pieces
RPG's continue to whistle overhead
Platoon sergeant calls Warlord AV unit for airstrike
McDougall runs over from bunker, gets hit in leg
KIA: Corporal James T. Jaspon
Medic runs over to him, too late.
(All we can do is fire back helplessly)

I cry alone in the bunker 'til morning light...

I have no dope
No matches—

No sense, no strength, no stamina, no appetite, no courage,
no thing
I seem to be nothing but eyes.

This writing is a waste of time—
This is the year 6067 in Vietnam.

    I dream I am the harbinger of peace. I wear the white
robe of purity—
    I walk through the jungle towards Hanoi...
    BRINGING THE MESSAGE OF PEACE.
    Only, when I get there I find they already know it.
    I walk along the causeway hitchhiking toward Washing-
ton D.C.
    BRINGING THE MESSAGE OF PEACE.
    When I get there, I find they already know it,
    (but nobody wants to sing it)
    They turn their faces away
    And talk about armament expenditures and research au-
thorizations and multilateral alliances and balances of power and multinational enterprises—
    To keep the wheels of the economy—
    Turning, Turning.

Letter to Sara

Sara: I know you must be busy, but when possible, write me please—

I stick it in a beer can and throw it in the blue, blue, blue sea.

The Buddhist Temple—
It looks, ahhhh, too beautiful to still be standing.

A wooden structure in a clearing in the jungle. Like a mirage on the horizon in the desert. Only it's tucked in the shade—a refuge beneath some trees. The wood is old and weathered but not rotten. Maybe it's teak or cypress of some sort. In the sides are painted Buddhas. One sits on a lotus flower with many arms and hands. Above the door are some symbols I don't understand.

My heavy boots echo around the room.
I nearly trip over the prone body of a Vietnamese guy who seems oddly and exactly my own age.
Is this really a Buddhist monk?
How come he doesn't move? Or look up—at me?
Doesn't he know I am the army of occupation?
Why does he keep lying on the floor?
DOESN'T HE KNOW I HAVE A GUN?!!

I feel like lying down on the cool wood floor in another corner of the quiet temple.
May I speak with Mahatma Gandhi please?

Or.......
I don't even care if I talk
Any more...
                    ...(the surrender)

The Vietnam Treaty
The Surrender of the Self.

(in order to surrender completely, first we must surrender everything—IN TIME AND SPACE)

(The time of war, this day in June...in what?)

(WHERE?)

(don't be surprised at the lack of rational order—for the random connections of these words follow the scientifically precise cosmic order of the universe)

I lie back upon the cool wood floor of the Buddhist temple.

(softly)
I ask myself what it is I must
SURRENDER

The answer comes

from within.

(very slowly)

I unlace the mile-long laces encircling my green jungle boots.

I walk slowly toward the front of the temple and place the two boots upon the altar.

Feeling the weight in my left hand, I look down to notice the battered black shape of an M16 automatic rifle. MAYBELLINE! Oh, no—not Maybelline!

What would happen, if...

If.........if?

Maybe it's not time yet.

I place Maybelline on the floor beside me.

She is not yet ready to leave.

Okay.

But still there is much to go.

Three canteens.

A pair of olive drab very dirty, very smelly socks. My jungle shirt.

I remove the wallet from my breast pocket.

I place the shirt on the altar.

I loosen my belt and the weight in the pockets easily surrenders my jungle pants. I bend down and remove the two cans of C-rations. One spaghetti and meatballs. One peanut butter and crackers.

The altar is filling up.

My heart is filling up.

I sit down upon the cool wood floor. My ass contracts from the cold.

Empty the contents of my wallet on the floor.

Geneva Convention card.

Connecticut drivers license.

Forty three Piasters.

Seven dollars Military Payment Currency.

Picture of Priscilla.

Picture of Sara.

Picture of Pensi.

Picture of my family.

Picture of Jesus.

Military Shot Record.

Draft Card.

Social Security Card.

Spare pack of matches—waterproof.

One dime.

Picture of me.

I only have to lean forward to reach a brass incense holder in which the above items are placed. I strike a waterproof match. It fizzles. On the seventh and last match the flame catches. Out of sentiment, I begin with my drivers license. For some reason it seems to carry the heaviest weight. Perhaps because it is the oldest of all the objects in the pile. It is dry and burns rapidly. I sprinkle the paper piasters onto the small flame and they catch fire in a burst. Then the rest.

I am lighter now.
I start to cry.
(it feels like a good sign)

Only my bandolier of ammunition and Maybelline remain.

The bandolier contains seven magazines, each containing eighteen rounds of M16 ammunition.

One by one, I pry the cartridges from the magazine placing them like candles along the step to the altar. The line eventually stretches the entire length of the step. They are brass and look beautiful in the light, which filters through the small windows in the temple.

Only Maybelline is left.

I remove her carrying strap.
I let her bolt slip forward one last time, placing her on SAFE.
Then I take her down.
The barrel.
The stock.
The bolt return spring.
Even her trigger mechanism.

MAYBELLINE IS DEAD.

Her broken pieces are placed upon the altar.
The cool breeze chills my naked skin.
I feel my pores breathe, at last.

My first smile: I look at the statue of Buddha and he smiles.

I feel a little awkward when the thought comes into my head: How should I sit?

Feebly, I try to bend myself into the posture that Buddha sits.

I think: I am copying Buddha's Way Of Sitting.

For some reason that seems important:

Buddha's Way Of Sitting.

I look behind me. The young monk now sits up.

He smiles.

I receive my second smile.

I turn my head back toward the altar, feeling embarrassed at my nakedness.

I close my eyes for refuge.

The first thing I think is that the monk is a faggot.

I feel ashamed at that thought.

So I compensate by thinking of Sara.

Then Pensi.

Then Sara again.

I feel foolish.

I tell my mind to be silent.

I feel the monk's hand upon my shoulder.

Lean forward, he says.

I don't open my eyes but do what he says.

I think if I open my eyes at this moment I might run from the temple.

I think of running up to the altar and assembling Maybelline as fast as I can (about four minutes) and slapping in a magazine of rounds and killing the monk.

My mind is going berserk.
I think, how can I stop?
The monk slips a pillow under my ass.
I sit back.

I think HOW CAN I STOP THESE THOUGHTS?
The monk says, think all your thoughts—they will pass.
It blows my mind.
He's reading my mind.
I need to get back to the LZ, I think.
Time is the smallest part of eternity, the monk says.
My body begins to shake so...I can no longer remain
sitting.
The monk pulls back on my shoulder and I lie back.
He walks away to the rear of the temple.
I hardly hear his footsteps.
I think of Pensi and start to get a hard-on.
Oh, no, I sit up and try to stop it.
I think of Buddha but
The hard-on grows larger.
Then I think, I just don't care.
What the fuck.
Why should it matter?
It goes away.
I lie back.
I AM WITH MY MEMORIES.

Thought beginnings
It's so cool in the temple.

The world for all its parts, for its green in this corner, its
bird flights of blue
    its tangerine nest of capitals, its smooth-scented deserts
    its crusted cracker mountains

female shaped valleys

Its palaces of spirit
cities I scoop up with a fingernail
sounds I listen to
smells I cut with a knife
it's light (which is) the
light of my eye

I create a picture of Sara and, really, her name is Sara.
And really she is beautiful beyond compare.

Still it is a world for my eating, not hers, and whatever
beautiful images it may contain of her, I shall be the judge.

I wish to offer cigarettes to her and vices.

When the white robe closes...

...when the sun shall come, those are the times the heart
shall be given...

Ambiguity is my forte. Ambiguity is the truth of the
artist.

He shall sometimes pretend not to pretend to pretend.

I have found you Sara on my tongue but shall lose you
(and pick you up again) as you cannot be swept away. I have
inherited your memory. You are my fortune. Stay in the
bearded castle with me, for-ever.

Again I feel the monk's hand on my shoulder. I sense
him leave something beside me. As he walks away, he makes
no noise, but I hear the door close.

I don't open my eyes.
(I put my hand down to touch what he's left—
—without opening my eyes)
(I feel a leaf—

THE MONK HAS LEFT ME A SINGLE LEAF UPON
A PLATE.
    —and I feel like—eating it)
    (is that a sin?
    is that a sin?)

I GET A WISH—
    what the monk
has left beside me is not a leaf
It is a giant plate of grass
    with a pipe
        to smoke it
        in—
        —in IN
        the cool
afternoon breeze
of the Va Bong Temple
Ba bong—
    I forget the words—
        —writ above the entrance
    the temple door—
        entrancing
        —so entrancing!—
        delighting
        joyous
        temple
        which
        is going—
   — inside me
        IS IT POSSIBLE FOR
—the temple
        to be going—
    inside me
????????????????????????????????

I roam the mountains like some foreign diplomat with his heart and mind and body intact. Watching the birth of some new universe inside me. The stars shine bright and I search—like reading an open book full of—so hard to grasp so much meaning so soon. The cricket's song elevates me. God's cool wind gives me the bliss of a friend. The sound of my feet on the ground brings me both backward and forward in time. The jasmine's smell hits me with waves of love. I feel the dried tears on my cheek and taste the ecstasy of sleep upon my tongue, and I feel sleep approaching like the tide of the China Sea. Sleep is now what must come, so now I lay myself down and now I sleep.

Death comes down like a drummer's sticks
In all variety of beats.

Three shells hit just outside my sight—
As if trapped on an island left to suffer,
I run directly toward the incoming rounds.

Zabriski is shaking his face in the mud—
(just when I step over his back
he picks up his head and in a businessman's
tone asks, do you think it's alright to go now?)

I run in my underwear in front of him
fast as a kid without shoes and
dive into a hole in the ground, naked, feet first.

Any questions to ask?
I look over at Zabriski
who is intent on reading the fear
on the face I reach up to feel is my own—

Behind me in the mud, O'Sullivan
counts his magazines.

The M60 machine guns spew their rounds, the bolts slamming back and forth like a typewriter carriage— thump, thump...silence: thump, thump, the frag's quick soundflashes, thump, crack, the hand flare drifts cautious-ly across the sky, moving across the world below in a slow minuet of turns, swish another flare replaces the five-second endless wait of darkness as the spark of the first flare dies in hell, crack! crack! so indelibly quick are the AK's. Booom the 4.2 tube pushes out its beauty, pop, the mortar flare brings its smoky glow down the steep trail in the sky, while in the faraway distance another grenade goes off and then another flare, putt, putt, putt, putt, putt, the 50's…crack, daatatatatatatata, the 16's to the left and then higher on the ridgeline, blam, blam, two more grenades, the sound is fury, the grenades explode one following another, two and three at the same time, in front, behind, left the 60 pushes quickly, the 16's are even faster, the story is written, to the left the 16's are snapping fast as snake tongues, the thumps of the grenades digging themselves into the dirt, so many men are standing, pulling the pins, one hand forward just quick enough to throw them, bringing the hand back for another, the man's short strong right arm pulls back on the bolt of the 50 and sets it off for another thump, thump, slow puff and every sound is frightening while thoughts are so quick and the eyes jump at a reason for any noise and the eyes burn with an intense pressure, the body temperature is hot and cold together, and it feels good to hurt your shin and knee to try to dig the bone into the rock and dirt to try to rub the skin off down to the quick because it seems that that is the person you are, with no flesh—only exposed muscle and…

Silence—

Always a silence.

It goes unnoticed at first and

Now Billy O'Sullivan, pass the name, is beyond the suffering.

I do not allow myself to dream. My dreams are cut in half by knives of fear. But even a crying man, through his fears, peers through the glaze on his eyes when everything then becomes holy.

Dear God—I know what I am.
But the light keeps going away.
I know I have thought every thought as a child,
And that I spend my life recounting my thoughts—
As slowly they drift back.

I sail across the American Landscape in a large purple hat.

America stretches out its huge body, its arms and neck, out toward the West like a huge sugar cookie. I walk across.

America, I don't remember you anymore.

This is the longest I've ever been away from your breast.

There is just enough light to see. I move my eyes down along the face of a leaf, following the red drop until it stops at the bottom edge, grows larger and falls.

A terrible feeling returns. I sit inside the mouth of a small black cave waiting for God to toss me a sizzling stick of dynamite. I shut my eyes tight then open them, blinking rapidly until the hurt changes into small floating purple dots that drift across my eyeballs.

My heart dances inside my shirt.

I am a tiny cast member in a huge cosmic production. The scenery is vast. The tree trunks are five feet in diameter. The leaves on the ground are a foot long. The boulders are the size of small houses. The forest smells of mold. Everything is decaying. This is where the world comes to rot and decompose.

I dream a dream of one girl
—but it turns out to be another.

A round, straw hat sails on the wind. It lands on the China Sea. And begins to sink. I dive after it. I am with the fishes again. They speak words that I feel but do not understand. I struggle but I cannot hear.

Tears from a million lights
Wash my buddies' hearts away.

Maybe if we looked into each other's eyes for a long, long time we would discover...
that
we must each just be
for ourselves, for all of the world

you
&
me

you   me

you
me

m
you
e

moyue

— The End —

Code of Conduct

1. I am an American fighting man. I serve in the forces which guard my country and our way of life. I am prepared to give my life in their defense.

2. I will never surrender of my own free will. If in command I will never surrender my men while they still have the means to resist.

3. If I am captured I will continue to resist by all means available. I will make every effort to escape and aid others to escape. I will accept neither parole nor special favors from the enemy.

4. If I become a prisoner of war, I will keep faith with my fellow prisoners. I will give no information or take part in any action which might be harmful to my comrades. If I am senior, I will take command. If not, I will obey the lawful orders of those appointed over me and will back them up in every way.

5. When questioned, should I become a prisoner of war, I am bound to give only name, rank, service number, and date of birth. I will evade answering further questions to the utmost of my ability. I will make no oral or written statements disloyal to my country and its allies or harmful to their cause.

6. I will never forget that I am an American fighting man, responsible for my actions, and dedicated to the principles which made my country free. I will trust in my God and in the United States of America.

Author's Note

Long Before the Next War was written when the author was 23 and just returned from Vietnam. The publisher suggested key cuts and revisions but the author never complied. When the publisher rediscovered the manuscript 45 years later and again contacted the author, the editing and the revisions were finally made. It seems 45 years was the time needed for the author to come to terms with his memories.

Tony Anthony, Author

Tony Anthony was born in New York. He served as a combat correspondent for the 198th Infantry Brigade in Vietnam in 1968 and 1969. His stories and photographs appeared in Stars & Stripes as well as in newspapers around the world. He was promoted to sergeant and received several medals including the Bronze Star for his reporting. He has written two previous books and directed a documentary film, Fearless Mountain, about a Buddhist forest monastery. He resides in Northern California.